THREE GOOBERS AND A NUT

A.T. Bugg

AKA/ Coach Randy Taylor

PublishAmerica
Baltimore

First printing

PublishAmerica has allowed this work to remain exactly as the author intended, verbatim, without editorial input.

ISBN: 1-60610-923-5
PUBLISHED BY PUBLISHAMERICA, LLLP
www.publishamerica.com
Baltimore

Printed in the United States of America

This book is in memory of Ruth Boggs Taylor, a sister-in-law who was more like a real sister! The love and understanding she showered on me was given as sister to brother, unselfishly and ever-present. Without her support and watchful eye, these writings would never have evolved.

To the many Goobers, also known as Friends, whose actions made these stories possible, Thank you for enabling me to return to a period of my life that was enjoyable and a foundation for life. These friendships have grown for more than 50 years! Some have ended with the passing of friends, but many continue as children of former Goobers cross paths with me.

The originals are alive and still kicking as Three Goobers and a Nut!

TABLE OF CONTENTS

THREE GOOBERS AND A NUT

In a place not too far from the past, just a short distance up the dirt roads of childhood, my friends and I pause to remember those days gone but not forgotten.

Shall we stretch our imagination and flex our mind to see those days once more?

These are the stories of "Three Goobers and a Nut". A collection of the training and preparation for life of four good, **NO,** We are today, Great friends, have been, and will be for life!!

To train a "Goober or a Nut" required a measure of good soil, the dirty kind, to rub on the face and hands. Also needed were lots of time, more than one teacher, lots of mischief, and above all, some good students!

It requires good wet muddy branches, the kind

that can be dammed up to make a hillbilly swimmin' hole, other creeks and ponds, to water the growing "goober". Plus, the water sources must provide entertainment, like fishing, swimming and skinny-dipping or moon bathing. Many a trainee has gone astray from the lack of dirt roads for adventure and travel. There must be fields of corn, to play in or to use as a hideout. Woods to explore, walk through, squirrel hunt, or just sit in and listen to the world swirl around them! Some times a trainee needs to be alone, especially if caught being a "Goober"; Other requirements: a watermelon patch, not your family patch, but a neighbor's! The best type of neighbor is the one that gets tore up from being the goat in a prank. Borrowing melons from them, without permission, usually does the trick! Anyone's barn loft, the best kind is full of bales of stacked hay and an endless supply of corncobs. These are necessary for throwing at each other in the battles of pride and war games. But the most important ingredient is WILLING TRAINEE's! Even with all these parts, the seasoning of a "goober" requires a daily dose of "The Three Stooges." This final touch is sort of like yeast in bread, something has to start the mixtures blending process!

Unfortunately, some "goobers" never grow up or reach the "nut" stage. I call these "Adults"!

These stories have taken place in arena not far from the heart, but deeply imbedded in the soul and mind of a different age! In this arena are dirt roads that wind and bump, but have no stop signs to interrupt, just the journeys and the roads of life that seem to go on for endless moments.

The Beginning of a Friendship: "How I Met Ollie Bay"

The "Old White Church" road wound past "Tipsy Old Boots" house, the edge of the "whispering woods," past Ole Hugh's barn and his "ghost like" woods, and joined a farm road at the wild cherry tree. At the connection of the two roads was a collection of sand that we used to fill burlap sacks for our bases. Some people used it to mix cement. The sand was a result of the sediments of runoff rainwater overflowing the road's ditches. It was about a mile and a half to my house from my cousin Dinks and Aunt B's house. Each place above made the walking distance shorter and the memories richer!!!!

I started home from Aunt B about mid afternoon on the Ole White Church road. As I top the rise, next to Uncle C's melon patch, I caught my first look of Ollie Bay and Hog, his little brother. Ollie was coming out of the "whispering woods" pushing the best-looking bicycle I'd ever seen! The woods were named by my brother to scare me into behaving, so my brother said! Mattie Lou, the snuff woman, lived down the road in the "whispering woods,"and was rumored to practice witchcraft! It seemed odd that two kids could come out of the "whispering woods" and not be scared! After all, the snuff woman wore a bonnet pulled down over her hair and all you would see were two scary eyes, peering out! Just thinking about her caused goose bumps all over me!

She was elderly, with dark teeth, covered in snuff and dripping from her chin.

When she laughed it sounded like a guinea cackling. She never said much, & kept to herself, so we figured she was evil, I guess.

Let's get back to meeting Ollie Bay. When he came out of the "whispering woods," and on to the Ole White Church road, our eyes met. Not sure of what to expect from each other, He stayed to the right and I stayed on the left side of the road. We kept walking!

Keeping a watchful eye on each other we moved

to the curve just south of "Tipsy Ole Boot's" house. Something was unusual about the way he walked. He had to push the bike, the chain was off! So as he walked I watched.

When we came to "Ole Hugh's woods and the farm road next to the woods, Ollie Bay took it. I stood watching him walk and then trot; he was trying to imitate, Uh...I know, it's Al Kaline of the Detroit Tigers! I had seen Al on Homerun Derby. OLLIE BAY was doing the Al Kaline homerun trot!

As he got to the corner of the woods, he must have seen or heard the ghost Tipsy Old Boots had told us about because he started to run.

In the summer time, the porch of the Ole Store at the Cross roads was the best place in the world for scary stories! (Those come later).

As he ran, I ran too, under the old mistletoe tree, past Ole Hugh's barn, toward the wild Cherry tree and the sand pile in the curve of the road.

What happened next was the start of a friendship that's stood the tests of time.

At the sand bar, Ollie bay arrived, Tater arrived, crash, boom, bang, thud!

Down we went, holding whatever part hurt the most!

The sand softens part of the fall!

Then I heard my first un-southern word.

"T hurts!" yelled Ollie Bay.

"What'd you say?" Tater asked.

"It hurts you hillbilly, can't you hear?" yelled Ollie Bay.

"Yeah, I hear, it just I ain't ever heard anyone talk so funny."

He sat up but didn't talk for several minutes, so I asked, "What's your name?" I'm Tater. I live at the crossroads. First house on the right passed Uncle Eulas' gristmill, where the big yard is!"

"I'm Ollie Bay, I live there." He said as he pointed at the big white house.

"Hey, that's where Trottin' Huey and Billy Beaver live," said Tater.

"Yeah, they're my uncles," said Ollie Bay.

With the knots on our heads and sand in our shorts, we had forgotten about "little hog." Here he comes pushing the bicycle. He's covered head to toe, in mud and smiling as if nothing were wrong.

"Daddy and Gem told you to stay out of the hog pen. Boy they're going to be mad at you," shouted Ollie Bay.

Tater took full advantage of the sand, practicing his slide while pretending there were bases to slide toward!

"Do you like baseball?" He asked.

"Sure do!" shouted Ollie Bay.

"Me too!" said the hog.

"Come up to the house, I'll show you some of my ball cards and a baseball from the stadium in Detroit," said Ollie Bay.

"Wow, I'm beginning to like you, even if you talk funny!" said Tater.

"Well, I'm beginning to like you too, sort of, you are funny sometimes especially when you talk." replied Ollie Bay.

When we got to Ollie Bay's house, Gem, their mother, wouldn't let little hog come inside.

Ollie Bay and I took turns spraying hog with the water hose. He liked that.

I knew then he wouldn't make a good goober! Too stubborn! But, he was a good baseball player, and I always picked him for my team. However, that's later!

That was how I met my friend, OLLIE BAY!!

An Ode to Wild Cat Willie

Wild Cat Willie was my Trainer and Mentor as I began to learn the paths, and finer techniques of being a Goober, as I grew up in the 1950's!

Wild Cat Willie dipped snuff, chewed tobacco, laughed often, worn a straw hat and could charm the fleas off the family dog!

His straw hat was covered in fishing lures and a bulge inside his hat revealed his snuff tin. These items plus his fishin' pole and a tin can full of worms were his most prized possessions! Man, he did love to fish!!!

His fishing trips required a stop at the Ole Mercantile Store at the Crossroads in Tenbroeck, (pronounced ten brook, and supposedly named for a racehorse that passed thru the area).

Uncle Pete, a local retiree and Veteran of WWII,

would always tease Willie with the statement, "Boy, I'm gonna eat them worms!"

Willie would usually hide his can of worms under the store's porch. I think it was more to keep the local dogs from tipping the can over and letting the worms crawl away than to keep Uncle Pete from eating the worms. Besides Uncle Pete was on a No Salt Diet and worms ain't good without salt! (I know I've tried 'em both ways)!!!!

Sometimes Willie would hide his worms in another place but in a week or so, he went back to hiding them under the porch again!

On this trip, Willie was having trouble finding a suitable hiding place for his can of worms. With Uncle Pete giving him the "evil eye" from the front porch of the store, Willie strolled to the barbershop side of the store, looking for a safe place for his fishing worms! There in the sand of the side parking area was three of his "goober trainees," shooting marbles! Rabbit, Uncle Pete's grandson, was lining up a shot. Dink sat on a wooden coke rack, rocking and waiting his turn to shoot! Tater came from back of the store, running, barefoot, doing his best to "Be like Willie," and buttonin' his overalls on the fly! Tater had been to the little building with the "part of the moon" carved out of the door. Or as that part is called today a "night light"!!!! (The outhouse)

When Willie saw Tater, a huge grin erupted and replaced the suspicious look on Willie's face. So big was the grin that if he had had lipstick on it would have touched both earlobes. Tater stopped, Rabbit and Dink looked at each other not sure what was about to happen next!

Willie walked over to Dink, reach down toward him, Dinks eyes grew to the size of, well let's say they got large from fright, and Willie placed his can of worms in the hole that the coke crate was supposed to cover! Dink thought Willie was after him!

Rabbit was so nervous that he started flapping his ear and singing! It was a Fats Domino song, "I found my thrill on Blueberry Hill!" Me, well I just turned a lot of red and could not talk. I mean Willie was my Hero!!! What could I say? Willie knew his worms would be safe with me.

With his worms safely hidden, Willie would lean his fishing pole against the store and disappear for a short time. When he got back, he was always covered with a powdery dust and spider webs in his hair.

Dusting himself off, he would brag, "I struck pay dirt," and show the coins he had found!

He had crawled under the store and found the coins that had fallen through the cracks of the stores floor.

It wasn't long before many of the local kids learn a lesson that all goober trainees would use: how to get a special treat.

We would crawl under the Ole Store and sift thru the dirt to try to find some coins. Not everyone had extra spending money then!

Willie raked the webs from his head, picked up his hat and went into the store. Inside was a world of things to meet the needs of the people in our community. There were bolts of cloth, needles, sewing boxes, thread, and thimbles for sewing quilts and dresses or shirts and blouses for the ladies. There were bins of nails and bolt; shovels, field hoes, and a collection of usable farm implements and other types of dry goods. All this and a MACHINE that kept coca colas, of all types, cold!!!!!

The rest of the stores goods surrounded the huge cash register. It must have had a hundred buttons to push, a huge crank style arm to ring up the sale, and a drawer for every button pushed. The fantastic part was the paper it printed, called a receipt, showed the amount spent and it didn't use a pencil!

While Willie was deciding what to buy, the owner Mr. Floyd P. was busy moving the register. Each spring and fall, he'd puff on his cigar and move the register. In the spring, he'd move up front so he could see the customers at the gas pumps. In those days, the owner usually pumped the gas. Another reason was to get close to the screen doors and the fresh cool air (no one had heard of air conditioning; and to some, electricity was a distant thought)!

In the fall, the register would go back toward the big potbelly stove so he could stay warm. Where the register was, coins could be found, under the building, when they fell thru the floor cracks. Cracks in the floor were a by-product of the wood having been put down fresh cut from the sawmill. As the wood cured or dried out it would shrink, thus the cracks in the floor!!

Willie's fishing trip would be special today. He had found a quarter and two pennies. He bought 5 pieces of bubble gum, a moon pie, and an RC cola with his money and had a dime left! If you are counting that's 1-cent per piece for the gum, a nickel for the moon pie, 6 cents for the RC and a penny tax!

Once outside he strolled up to the three of us rubbed my head and gave each of us a piece of bubble gum. We were now Goobers for life.

I can see Wild Cat walking up the dirt road, fishing pole, a can of worms, and his treats going to Big Luke's pond, to catch what ever came his way!

It's easy for me to remember Wild Cat but I want to describe him for all to see. So please daydream a little bit and enjoy the trip with me!

His muscles were hard as a rock, and he had a touch of Tom Sawyer in him. He was always running into trouble. Mostly he just ran. He would run anyone or anything! He ran every chance he got, and always barefooted!

The roads were all dirt. Gravel was very rarely used, too expensive! So the soft dirt road was easy on the feet.

He could outrun all the guys, even the older ones. About the only thing that could challenge him was the guard dog at Old Rocky's Garage. Wild Cat would dangle a red bandana from his back pocket. Then he would run by the garage and holler at Old Chino, the guard dog. The dog would chase Willie and I swear the dog would grin as he chased Willie. I think they both enjoyed the fun of boy against dog!

Wild Cat built his muscles by lifting the sacks of fertilizer, seeds, and feed at the farm supply shed. His uncle, Big Barn, worked there and he never missed a chance to rest if Wild Cat Willie was around to work for him!

If business was slow, in the afternoon, Big Barn would let us kids and Wild Cat stack the one hundred-pound bags of seed on a steel cart and roll the cart to the front of the shed. At the front of the shed, we were allowed to build a fort by stacking the bags.

Big Barn was smart, like a fox! He knew the farmers always waited until late in the day to pick up their products. So he would let us load the cart and roll it to the front for him. He stood by and pointed to the bags he wanted put on the cart. Strange, the bags were just what the farmer needed that afternoon!

Anyway, we got to play in the shed and Big Barn got the bags moved up front.

As spring began to arrive, the Tom Sawyer in Willie began to show! He hated to be inside. If there was a chance to miss school, he took it, even if he had to work in the fields.

The only time I ever remember him wanting to go to school was the time our teacher gave him a part in the spring play. He had to be there to practice his part with others. The play, "Wild Cat Willie Saves the Day," gave him his nickname!

His lines "I'm rough, I'm tough, and I always tell the truth, or my name ain't Wild Cat Willie." He got to put a dip of snuff in his lip and carry his rifle in the play.

Willie enjoyed being the center of attention and the play was his time to shine!

The play was in his sixth grade year and in the summer, he when to a Great Foot Race in Heaven.

I can see him fishing with the Great Fisher of Men, resting after running on the streets of Glory!

Willie died that summer when a tractor, with a cotton poisoning devise, rolled over and landed on him!

OLD BOB

Old Bob came into my life on my sixth birthday. He was a liver spotted German short hair bird dog. I got to play with him a lot. He'd crawl upon my back when I would lay on the ground. Licking my ears and face, biting at my hair, or pulling my pants leg, these were, according to my dad, territorial things. That was how an animal determines his rank of power. I just knew he played hard. I didn't care about where he stood in rank. I had a playmate and it turned out for life.

He followed me every place I went. He tried to do anything our guys did. So naturally, he went along as a "goober." (Goober—a term applied to the younger guys I ran around with and the strange adventures we experienced in our community. Some caused by nature, others by mistake, and those that took genius to prepare and pull off.)

Old Bob followed me to the edge of the road, where I met the school bus. But, he had to learn to stay back as the bus left him. It didn't take many commands of No! Stay! Also, the switch across his back legs, from my Dad, helped him learn what to do. As he got older, he would meet me as I got off the bus in the afternoon, at the Ole store.

I made a rag ball to training him to retrieve. I couldn't throw too far but it was just right for his short legs. His legs, muscles, and intelligence all grew very rapidly. It wasn't long before he could catch the ball before it hit the ground.

He began to run, with his nose on the ground and his tail pointing skyward, he was trailing something! Dad said it was a natural part of his bloodline. I didn't understand, I just wanted him to play ball with me!

Before long, I had to switch the rag ball, for a baseball and my bat. He could run farther than I could throw. But I could hit farther than I could throw. So I would hit the ball, Old Bob would run it down, bring it back, drop the ball, and sit! If I tried to pick it up, he would grab it and run!

Not good! If he were to do that in the field when hunting, no telling what might happen! Many good dogs had been shot for things like that! I had to provide something to get him to leave the ball. It was spring. I needed a treat, but what? It was strawberries! That dang dog would eat strawberries!

Mother didn't think too much of it. She made jam from those berries! The last thing she needed was to have to go to Aunt B's for extra strawberries! BUT, I trained Old Bob to fetch a ball for a strawberry!

Bird dogs had to earn their keep! I mean they had to produce, something useful or we didn't keep them. That something Old Bob provided was food, in the quail's Dad would hunt!

Bob white quail is one of the best tasting foods anyone could consume. It just happened my Dad was one of a group of the best Quail hunters in the county.

Dad made sure I didn't ruin him; Old Bob would hunt first, and then be my playmate!

My Dad trained Old Bob very carefully, bringing him along slowly, with stern directives. His training and skills were exhibited often for anyone who had the good fortune to hunt with my Dad.

It didn't take long for the news about his talent and bloodlines to spread to the hunters.

Dad even went to extremes with the fetch and carry training. Using my grandmother Bertha's leftover biscuits, he taught Old Bob to pick up a 2-gallon milk bucket and bring it to the house. Dad put different amounts of things in the bucket to be sure Old Bob could carry the load.

One day a cousin, and a man, looking for a good hunting dog, came to visit. They were in for a treat. My grandmother told them if they could follow a bird dog, they could find my Dad in the field. She put a bucket handle in Old Bob's mouth. In the bucket was a jug of cold water for us in the field!

She told Old Bob "take the bucket to Tater," (that's my nickname) and the men followed in amazement.

Old Bob led the men to a shade tree, on the edge of the field, where my dad and I sat.

Once in the field the men talked business, the purchase of a bird dog. It scared me, because I thought they wanted Old Bob. They got the next best thing, a puppy from Cricket and Old Bob's union. Cricket was Dinks' favorite dog, just like Old Bob was mine. When you care for an animal as we did as kids, they became more like family members. (Dink is my cousin but we were raise more like brothers)

Having watched my Dad use the scent of quail feathers to teach Old Bob to trail and retrieve, it seemed like a good idea to teach him to retrieve all types of balls using the same method.

Uncle Eulas G. raised birddogs also. He also kept a pen of bob white quail. That meant quail droppings. I got a bag of dirt from the quail pen and made a kind of a rosin bag. I used it to rub all the balls. Touch the ball and you had the scent of a quail. Nobody, in the game, ever figured out why Old Bob was always sniffing the guys during a game.

I just laughed, sitting on the ground with my bag of dirty deeds! About the only way to get rid of the scent was Lava hand soap! Can you imagine a pitcher tossing a spitball before he found out about the dirt? (ha/ha) (I never told anyone until now—sorry Rabbit but you always had a lot of ball movement without the bird—uh spit)!

Old Bob made a great hunter and I had a great playmate and pet. He helped invent knee high nighttime baseball equipment. Well, that might be stretching it a bit. But, without his nose, it might not have been possible for me to get the ball-bats we used.

I'd take him with me to the ball games on Saturday and Sunday afternoon when the local independent teams played close by.

It took some talking, but I usually convinced the person we rode with that Old Bob needed to go. Besides, who would watch me while the game was played?

At the game, I would stroll up to Bonny H., Connie Mack, Curly, or Cokamoe, the team spark plug. These were the team's best hitters! I would offer to chase their homerun or foul balls for a nickel, or any broke bat they didn't want.

Maybe it would be Ned Mc., Lefty Don T., or "Tracks" as he was later known, Mr. Magoo, R.C., Big "V," or the "crafty" George Edward, that pitched. I would make the same type of deal with them.

The baseballs were used until they wore out because teams couldn't afford a new ball after a foul, like in the major leagues. Many of the players would purchase a baseball or two to help the team. Naturally, each player wanted his baseball returned after the game.

First, I would find the bag of baseballs and rub my dirt bag on all of them. Then if a ball went into the woods, or a field of corn, Old Bob would find it for me. (Playing at Mt. Flat, it was a ground rule double when the ball went into the corn). A lot of the players would run into the tall corn, find the ball, and wave their glove and the ball as if they had made a catch for an out! There was always a discussion (another word for a fight) after that because the umpire most always favored the home team.

The first ruling was NO catch if it was the visitor and an OUT if it was the home team. So the managers decided on a ground rule double if the ball was hit into the cornfield!

Too much corn was knocked down over a ball game! So, if the ball went into the cornfield it had to be found by someone other than the outfielder. That's when old Bob went to work!

Old Bob found the ball easily and quickly, always dropping the ball at my feet.

Sometimes the teams sold food and drinks to help pay the umpire. So if I built up the number of baseballs returned to five, I got a candy bar, ten got a cold sodie (pronounced soda) water (slang for coca cola, 2-way, 7 up, Nehi grape, or orange crush) and Old Bob wanted his share! He loved the ice that was left on the drink bottle.

The bottles were glass, with metal caps that required an opener to pop the cap off. We saved the caps and played stickball with them. Try hitting a bottle cap curveball with a broom handle bat!

Mostly it was chase the ball for a broken bat.

Those bats became our knee high nighttime bats. Because of Old Bob, I had a large collection of broken bats!

Old Bob was around 15 years of age when Uncle C. found him hanging in a fence near one of the fields we had hunted for quail.

I think he went hunting by himself, tried to jump the fence, and got caught in the top strand. I guess with as many fences he crossed, he figured one more wasn't any different.

Happy hunting Old Bob!

GOOBERS IN TRAINING

Every kid in the community had a fantasy of what he wanted to be as an adult. Mine was to play major league baseball, in Yankee Stadium.

I've heard it said that imitation is the greatest kind of flattery a person gets in life. All the kids in our neck of the world picked a baseball player to imitate.

Ollie Bay ran like Al Kaline, the hall of fame outfield of the Detroit Tiger. I learned to switch hit and started out at shortstop, just as Mickey Mantle had done. I even wore his number, 7!

Rabbit wanted to be Whitey Ford, but he couldn't throw left-handed, so he learned throw a screwball. It broke into a right hand batter and away from a left hand hitter!

That left Ole Dink to pick from all the others, sort

of a utility player, so he got to be whoever he could think of that game!

Y'all got to remember there were only eight teams in each league in the late 50's. That's 16 total, and none of them were west of the Mississippi River, except the Cardinals of St. Louis!

We knew players chewed tobacco to keep their mouth moist and to keep from drinking too much water! We all started out chewing bubble gum from the ball cards packets we bought. Then someone snatched some "Bull of the Woods," a brand of chewing tobacco!

Nature took its course!

Someone took a chew from the tobacco and passed it on to the next goober, me!

Not wanting to look foolish, as if I needed anything to reveal that point, I took a huge bite of the tobacco plug! I started to chew.

About the second or third time my teeth met, the sting of tobacco juice seasoned my tongue and cheek. My eyes began to water and my nose started to drip, and I slobbered a lot. Some people say they spit, not me! I foamed at the mouth, gurgled, heaved, croaked, coughed, sneezed, and then it got worse.

The game began with me at shortstop. Ollie Bay

was pitching, and giggling about me! He said I looked like a small version of the Jolly Green Giant, only I didn't have to use the suit to be green! I had swallowed the juice produced from chewing the tobacco.

Ollie Bay threw a pitch.

Dink closed his eyes, swung, and nailed me with a liner!

I never saw the ball, but it found me. When the ball plunked me, I must have swallowed. We never found the plug of tobacco.

I didn't play ball or anything else for two or three days.

Rabbit and Dink came by to visit, but I didn't have time to talk to them. I was too busy answering nature's call, in the bathroom!

Rabbit told Dink, later, that he had never seen me move that fast before. Dink said he figures it was the tobacco juice that increased my speed and wondered if I was going to keep using it to help my speed on the base paths. They were laughing as they left. I wondered if it was about me. Because I was already thinking about what to do as a pay back for their fun and my —-got to go again—darn tobacco—misery!

Dink and Rabbit left Tater's yard laughing and

talking very secret like. As they headed toward Rabbit's Grandmother's for something to eat, his favorite past-time second only to breathing, an old habit over took Rabbit. He began to slap his ear and sing. It was a Fats Domino song, "I'm walking to New Orleans."

When he got nervous, this strange habit kicked in and he slapped his ear until it turned red!

Or, he got his tail spanked by his mother. Which ever came first!

Dink asked, "Rabbit, what the heck are you so nervous about?"

Rabbit replied, "Tater's up to something. I get this nervous twitch when he's up to something."

"We didn't do anything to him." said Dink.

"We laughed at him," said Rabbit.

Well, it was funny. They agreed on that as they walked.

What Tater had in store for the three goobers (Ollie Bay, Dink, and Rabbit) would take special plans. Tater had plenty of time to decide what he would do. He spent the next 4 days, making trips to the bathroom, answering false alarms at one end, coughing, and saying something about that would be the last time he'd chew tobacco, at the other!

THE SNOWMAN

The most fun in the late fall and on into winter was a snowfall. Sometimes it was enough to close the schools in the county for a day, or if we were lucky, for several days.

Naturally, no one wanted us in the house.

Where did we go? What to do? Where else? The Big Yard at Tater's! Here was some of the finest and most artistic snow to be found!

Starting at the drainage tile in his driveway, Aunt Bell (everyone in the community called her that and she was Tater's Mom) had just widened the driveway in the summer, as if she expected it to snow. She could convince most anyone to go along with her ideas. So, she talked the county road crew into giving her several chipped ditch tiles; Then she talked them into loading them in a county truck, hauling them to the Big Yard, and unload them in our ditch beside the main driveway. Then again, it might have been the fried apple pies and iced tea she just happened to have in her truck when she found the men replacing the tiles. Either way she got her tiles.

She wanted a wide driveway for the different farm equipment to be able to get in the yard to turn around in without messing up her lawn! Most likely, it had something to do with the fact she couldn't see if a car was coming when she backed out of the drive! A wider drive allowed her to turn around in the yard and see if there was traffic on the road.

Now where was I? The ditch where the snow would drift into three or four foot depths, allowed us to start with a small ball and add layers of snow. When the snowball got to be difficult to roll, we would have our base for the snowman. We rolled two or three more balls of snow for the body and the head.

Now the fun part of snowman building. Splitting into two groups, Rabbit and Dink went one way and Ollie Bay and Tater went the other. Who would find the finishing touches to make the snowman look real?

Forty-five minutes or so later, the two teams met at the site! Dink had a four-prong rake. Rabbit had a leaf rake. These were to be the arms of Mr. Snowman! Ollie Bay had a sack like tote bag with newspapers stuffed inside the bag.

What imagination, a paperboy snowman!

I found a ball cap for his head, several chunks of coal, for teeth and eyes, and a carrot for his nose. But, he wasn't finished, something wasn't right.

I had an idea. He would need to RELIEVE himself, so I fixed his plumbing with an OUTLET! A three-foot section of two-inch black drainage pipe was inserted in the snowman and his arms (the rakes) were positioned as if holding something!

Planning was a necessary evil of being a "goober". So, when we started the project we rolled the snowball toward Aunt Fanny's house. She was the widow lady across the road. We enjoyed doing things that got her attention. Let me tell you she could get tore up at almost nothing. Like the times when someone would sneak up on an unsuspecting victim and pull his pants down to his knees, thereby mooning her.

Of course, this only happened if she fussing at us for hitting a baseball toward her huge picture window!

In all the games played in the Big Yard, my house got more broken windows than all three of the others in the neighborhood. Those three houses were just part of our playing field.

If a ball hit Aunt Rosie's house, her good-looking daughter would throw the ball across the road! She would have been a good athlete but her hooters hindered her throwing motion.

If it was my grandmothers' house, she would tell us to hit it the other way. Naturally, the other way was toward Aunt Fannie's house!

True, we did stomp down a few (dozen) flowers and maybe a fruit tree or two! But, they always grew back the next year.

Well it's "gettin' tore up" time for Fanny!

We left the snowman with the finishing touches for Aunt Fanny; but to make sure our creation was seen we stood along side the road and pointed him out to several cars as they drove by!

It took about five minutes for her to see what's facing her window.

Here she came toward Aunt Bell's house; stomping through the snow, arms waving, foam and snuff spewing from her mouth, as she shouted about what those boys had done!

By that time, we were long gone. We headed

towards the clubhouse, in the woods, in front of Granny C's house.

She was Rabbit's grandmother. She would try to be our alibi, but would give our secrets away! She would be laughing about what we had done and everyone knew we were GUILTY!

For at least the next two weeks, at the Old Store, talk was about the snowman in Tater's yard!

No one, but me, got in trouble. That the thanks I got for the on-the-job training of the "goobers."

Next time we build a snowperson, I'll put a bucket on its head and a beach towel around its waist. That way those who do not appreciate creative art can guess, or lift the towel to be sure before repeating idle gossip, or as Joe Friday would say, "just the facts ma'am, just the facts!"

ON THE FROZEN POND

The winters of the late 50's and early 60's were cold enough to freeze the small pond at Uncle John L's. Not just a coat of ice, but solid enough to support several knuckleheads trying to play Ice Hockey!

The pond wasn't more than three or four feet deep at any point. It was used to water the animals in the pasture of the farm Uncle C. rented. He also cultivated by rows the land of Uncle John L.

Among the cattle grown on the pasture, Willie D. had a horse called Old Red. Red pulled a small wagon and a buggy that Willie D. used to take the girls riding at community socials and church picnics.

On that day, the "goobers" were watching Willie D. feed Old Red. Red wasn't many hands tall, but he was stoutly built. Red was something similar to a small Clydesdale or Belgium breed, and was smart as well as strong. Willie D. loved to show the things Red had mastered. Willie would ask Red if he wanted something to eat. Red would paw the ground two or three times as he shook his head up and down. Given some grain, Willie D. would ask Red "will you help me get on and take me for a ride?" Red would shake his head yes. Willie D. would walk in front of Old Red, with his back to the horse, and part his legs. Willie D being six foot and six inches tall made it easy for Old Red to put his head and neck between Willie D's legs. With a quick upward thrust of Red's head Willie D. was on Red's back! Red started toward the pond, when Dink yelled, "let's go break the ice, Red wants a drink of water!"

The real reason we were at the pond was to bust the ice near the edge of the pond. This was to let the animals get some water.

Willie D. just had to test the thickness of the ice. He walked on to the edge of the ice and stomped!

Nothing happened!

He went a few feet further onto the ice and began to slide or skate! Anyway, he was moving!

One by one, we edged onto the ice and made weak efforts to skate.

Tater got a pine limb, to try to lean on and not fall. Tater had a huge corncob in his coat pocket, probably to start a cob battle if things got dull!

Rabbit, Dink, K.T., Hands, and Ollie Bay had watched Tater use the limb, so they all got one! Bernie had waited until everyone else had gotten on the ice before he joined the game!

He was always on Willie D's side!

Ollie Bay had lived in Detroit and had been to some hockey games. So, when the cob fell out of Tater's pocket and onto the ice, he yelled "Slap shot!"

He drew his stick, the limb, backward, then swung, and smacked the cob! The cob skimmed across the ice and Dink tried to chase it!

The others made feeble attempts to move! But you would have had to seen Rabbit to enjoy the beauty of it all as he did his version of Curly, of the Three Stooges, with his shoe nailed to the floor, turning circles!

He had one foot planted and the other slipped as he attempted to move, causing him to go in a circle! Dink took a step or two, fell, and began to laugh pointing at Rabbit.

"He's doing donuts," said Dink.

Rabbit said, "at least I'm still standing up!"

K.T. was easily the best skater! He adjusted to the ice by using his roller skating skills.

All of us, except K.T. and Ollie Bay, slipped and fell more times that Jimmy Carter has teeth. We tried to go too fast. That doesn't work on ice!

Bernie sneaked on to the ice, near the Cob and used a shovel as his stick! He had been leaning on it while watching Willie D and Old Red.

Bernie scooped the puck, (shoot I mean the cob), slung it across the ice and yelled for Willie D to get it and score!

Willie D. began to slide toward the cob. As he picked up speed, he didn't see the clump of wiregrass sticking about four or five inches above the ice!

The grass was frozen stiff and when Willie's boot contacted the grass, it flipped him into the air! He weighed about 150 pounds, but he went into the air, straight up and straight down! His butt hit first and busted the ice! All of him went under water!

All of us made our way off the ice.

Willie D. struggled to get to side of the pond, mostly crawling. By the time he reached the bank of the pond, every thing he had on was frozen!

Shaking from the cold, Willie started toward his house. It was about a quarter a mile from the barn! Each stride resembled Frankenstein and his hair looked like a tall Don King, or maybe the fin on a blue marlin! His arms stuck out like a scarecrow and his pants looked like Aunt B had used too much starch on washday!

The good thing about falling thru the ice was no one had to work at watering the rest of the cattle. They helped themselves where Willie D crawled out of the pond!

Bernie put the shovel in the barn. Ollie Bay and K.T. were arguing about how high Willie D went into the air. Rabbit, Dink, and Tater were performing their famous act of the Stooges!

We waded thru the dusting of snow; maybe an inch or so, hoping Aunt B had lots of hot cocoa to drink!

We were all cold but not like Willie D.!

KING OF THE MOUNTAIN, COB BATTLES, GREEN PLUMS, AND ROTTEN EGGS

Some of the games we played as kids, usually involved a certain amount of rough play. The following is a brief story (maybe that's stretching the truth a little) about goobers and the older Nuts, of a place known as Ten yards of Truth and a few feet of your imagination.

Not everyone had a huge pile of corncobs in their backyard, but I was lucky!

Just beyond the garden and across the branch (that's a fancy description for a ditch) was the grain and feed mill. All the corn gathered by the local farmers was brought here and sold to Pony, the owner of the mill.

As the corn was shelled, a huge blower would shoot the cobs and shucks through a metal tube and into an area behind the mill. Some of the farmers would load the fresh cobs and shucks on their wagons to use as feed for cattle. But most of the fresh cobs and shucks were left to rot into compost for fields and gardens.

The cobs and shucks were heated as the corn was shelled. The smell of fresh corncobs would cause the cattle on a farm to go crazy, even to the point of trying to climb into the wagon before the cobs were unloaded!

We were warned not to play on the cob pile, especially while the mill was operating; but do goobers ever listen? No!

We would climb the side of the cob pile that no adult could see. Then jump into the path of the cobs and shucks coming out of the metal tube! The force of the air, plus the shucks and cobs, would send us tumbling down the pile of cobs!

After two or three trips to the top of the cob pile, some goober would declare himself King of the Mountain. Another goober would try to knock, throw, push, or pull him off the mountain! The rest of us would throw cobs at HIM! If we were lucky, another "Nut" would take his place! Then we could pepper his head with the cobs!

Since we were always taking sides (that's

country for choosing teams) the battles would, and did get heated! A well-thrown cob could sting a goober or one of the other team members! That's all it took and the Battle of the Century, week, day, or what ever was in gear!

The number on the teams in the battle was determined by who was at the cob pile.

Trotting Huey (referred to in other tales as Dudt') was the only odd piece of the war games! If he was in the battle, it was five against four, or three against two!

During one of the games, on the cob pile, someone hit Trotting Huey on the side of the head, with a very rotten smelly corncob! He swore it was Billy Beaver who threw the cob, but to this day, I can tell it wasn't him! I know—it took my best throw!

This act of courage set off a feud that made the neighborhood gossip column! We didn't have a newspaper but we did have a lot of loose Lips!

That strange curled lip, those goofy looking eyes, rolling and squinting, signaled the wheels in Huey's mind were plotting revenge!

Probably the most memorable part of this continued battle from the cob pile, was the Cornstalk City Gang (Bill Beaver and Hog) plus

Bernie and Willie Dee, against the Dis-hottles (Rabbit and Dink), Trotting Huey, plus the Goober Trainers (Tater and Ollie Bay).

Hog and Beaver often hid in the cornfields to attack unsuspecting victims! They used maypops, cobs, clods of dirt, plums, apples, peaches, watermelon rinds, muskmelons, or squash, and especially over ripe cucumbers, anything that could be thrown as ammunition.

This particular battle broke out when Trotting Huey stumbled upon Hog and Beaver building a hideout in the cornfield!

Huey gets this brainstorm. He wants to pull one on the Beaver, call it revenge for telling their Mom that Huey had sneaked off in the car to see his girl!

(Trotting Huey is called Huey for the rest of the story) Huey wanted to use overripe tomatoes as ammunition. He used bribery to get Ollie Bay and me to go along with his hit and run attack.

He told Ollie Bay that it might leak out that Ollie Bay was building pyramids using beer cans in the front yard of a certain girl on Saturday nights! Purr, Ollie's girl, wasn't exactly thrilled either, even though she enjoyed the attention she got from Ollie Bay! So, he went along with the attack on Hog and Beaver.

Huey said he knew who put the watermelon in Suzy Q's mailbox, so I had to go along, too! Her dad wasn't amused with the melon prank. It took him about an hour to cut the melon out of the mailbox, wash the juice and seeds from the box, and then wipe it dry before the mail was delivered! (More on the watermelon later)

Little did we know about a surprise that was waiting to unfold on us! We would all be plum surprised!

Huey had hid in the cornfield and had shot his older brother Bernie with a BB gun. Bernie swore to get even with Huey (revenge comes later). Bernie could hit rabbits or any moving object with his slingshot (that's a fancy word for a flip). Huey's surprise comes later!

Each one of us took a bushel basket to the tomato patch and filled it with overripe and/or rotten tomatoes! We sneaked into the woods a short distance from Cornstalk City and waited.

Out of the cornfield came Billy Beaver, followed by Hog. Huey opened up, with a softball size, rotten tomato and a direct hit to the face of Billy Beaver!

Hog turned to run and got hit several times by the tomatoes Ollie Bay and I threw!

Beaver and Hog ran back into the cornfield and

circled behind me. They sneaked upon me and knocked the basket from my grasp. Armed with our tomatoes, they began to chase us! Huey turned and ran. We followed him, with tomatoes glancing off our heads and backsides. Not far behind us were two screaming examples of being "Mad as a Hornet," Hog and Beaver!

Huey ran into the barn, climbed into the hayloft and hid in the bales of stacked hay! He didn't have anything to throw at Hog and Beaver, so he tried to hide from them.

The goobers (me and Ollie Bay) made a detour through the plum trees to the back of the barn. Ollie Bay and I just barely got into the loft when Huey crawled out of the hay. Just in time for about four pounds of fresh, overripe, juicy, red tomatoes to splatter all over him. Both of us were about to wet our pants from laughing so hard.

Huey swore a couple of times, reached into a hen's nest and removed two or three eggs. (If you lived on a farm, raising chicks was a moneymaking project. The pen was put in the hayloft to make it more difficult for wild varmints to get in to. If the eggs weren't hatched, they spoiled or turned rotten! The odor of a rotten egg is a sulfur smell.) Now armed with something to throw, Huey waited for Beaver or Hog to get close enough for him to throw at them.

Beaver walked between a trailer and the wall of the barn. He snagged his blue jeans on a nail! He couldn't go anywhere! Huey always liked any advantage he could get!

None of us were prepared for what exploded on the scene next!

Huey cackled, and threw the rotten eggs, one, two, three, and just like bombs, they exploded all over Beavers' head and clothes!

Beaver went Nuts! Screaming, crying, and slapping his face like Curly of the Three Stooges, he ran pulling his jeans off, then his shirt and finally his underwear.

Huey sensed trouble when he heard his Mom scream for everyone to come to the house. Knowing he would get grounded or worse, Huey tried to bribe me to say I had hit Beaver with the eggs. That didn't work, so he used psychology on me; when he said, "I'll beat you up," that worked.

Climbing down the hayloft steps, we heard Bernie say to Huey, "I've got you!"

Huey ran out the back of the barn, trying to get away from Bernie.

The Dink-Dishottles were behind a cattle feeder

waiting to unload their corncobs on somebody! They peppered Huey.

He turned to go to the fruit trees for cover and there stood Bernie!

Flip pulled back and put a green plum in the pouch as ammo! He fired the plum toward Huey. Wham, a solid hit on the forehead of Huey! He did a complete flip and landed in the mud below!

Willie Dee and Hog were sitting under the plum trees. Willie had stepped on a board that had a nail in it. Lucky it went in to the heel of the boot he was wearing! Hog was tugging at the board, a weak effort, to pull it lose from the boot!

I think the effort was weak because of all the laughing they were doing at the happenings around the barn!

Bernie lost his driving license for 2 weeks. Huey was knocked out and lost the battle of Cornstalk City; and I was banned from playing at their house for two weeks. Dink and Rabbit were on the run. Ollie Bay was peeping around the corner of the barn giggling at all the wounded, limping, and otherwise marked warriors. Plus, I had to wash Beaver's clothes to get the smell out of his jeans.

That took some doing because I had to tell mom what happened. I had to mow our yard by myself, twice, as punishment. That wouldn't have been so bad but all of our baseball games at my house were stopped also! All this plus I had to walk the ¾'s of a mile home.

But the fun ain't done yet!

To get home I had to choose, walk by the home of Big "H" and Little "B," the fox hunting brothers, and take a chance they weren't sitting of their front porch. If they were, that could lead to a huge dose of teasing. Which I could do without, from both of them and their very loud and annoying sister! Or, I could pass thru Tipsy Ole Boots' woods and go by Granny C's house and pray she didn't see me!

If Granny saw me, there would always be a good laugh as she told and retold the story about Tater and his dirty underwear on a stick! Oh, I forgot to mention I carried the clothes on a long stick! Yuck!

I made it to our yard and almost got the clothes into a washtub. But, Old Bob told on me. His barking and howling caused everybody to come out of the house when he took a sniff of the clothes on the stick!

Dink and Rabbit had tucked tail and ran to Maw Maw's house when Huey got hit with the green plum. Here they came howling with laughter and pointing at me.

Mother made me take a bath in the yard! She had me use lava soap, tomato juice, and a coldwater hose to rinse off everything. None of this bothered me, except the two Dis-hottles' howling laughter! I'll get them if it takes a hundred years!

THE HUNTERS

In the early 50's, the type of job was farming for the majority of the area work force. A few worked in the small towns as a waitress, sales person, or maybe a delivery driver.

But, as I think back to that time, there were several men who never seemed to work. They were always sitting on the porch of the Ole Country store. Usually swapping stories and whittling on a piece of cedar. Some of the stories were about World War II.

However, if big Hub and /or little Bill were at the store a prank of some kind was being planned. These two would do almost anything to anyone at anytime! They loved sports and must of hated work because neither had a steady job!

At night they hunted, at least they took their hunting dogs along to increase the possibilities that it might seem like were hunting.

Once the camping area was set up, the dogs were turned loose! Lanterns were hung, and a fire was built. It helped provide enough light to see the cards being dealt. A pot of coffee was in the making as the big urn hung over the fire. A poker game was always used to pass the time as the dogs ran or trailed a fox or maybe a raccoon. If the trail was hot, that means a strong scent of an animal was being followed, the sound of the dogs barking, as they trailed, would make you sleepy!

One time, at the Ole store, little Bill offered me a nickel to pull his finger! Not knowing any better, I did and he raised his leg and broke wind. It roared and all the ones on the porch roared with laughter. Then the men got a second laugh. I offered him my finger! When he pulled my finger, I broke wind!!

Big Hub and little Bill lived with their spinster sister big Lu. She was loud and large. She had a lap dog named Chino. He was supposed to be a small dog but he got feed from the table and he ballooned. He weighed almost 25 pounds. He was like his owner, very large for his size. His weight must have adjusted his attitude, from sociable to antisocial, because he barked and growled at everything!

Once Granny C, Rabbit's grandmother, had the

three of us, Rabbit, Dink, and me, take some vegetables to Big Hub, Bill, and Lu.

Granny had a very big garden and shared with everybody in the neighborhood. We slowly walked up to screened in porch when out of the blue charges a 4-legged, bowling ball shaped, barking, growling, slobbering at the mouth—uh uh guard dog! He was moving too fast to control his forward motion (lard can butt) smashing nose first into the door. The door had a piece of wood attached to protect the screen from being scratched and torn. We almost dropped the vegetables when the dog ran at us, but when Big Lu yelled at Chino to get back and shut up, I jumped behind a bush and went ten/ one hundred!(wet myself) Rabbit froze and Dink just leaned on the wall breathing hard, holding his chest!

She motioned us in to the house. I looked everywhere for the dog. All I saw was three or four metal dishpans, covered with cloth. The shades were pulled so most of the light was blocked out.

What was in those pans? Before I could look under a cloth, Ole Chino sneezed, growled, and farted as he ambled over to his bowl of Coke, not water, but Coca-Cola. Spoiled beyond repair was this animal!!!

wiggled a little, but she just tightened her grip. She handed me two half dollars as she sprayed my shoe with perfume.

That was just what I needed to add to the smells on me already. Try describing what a sweaty, young guy, who had just been peed on by a dog, carried cucumber, squash and beans in his arms would smell like! Add to that the odor of a woman who dipped snuff and slept with a fat dog, (neither had bathed in forever!) Just think raunchy and then beyond. My dog, Old Bob, wouldn't get around me until I bathed!

Later Rabbit told us that when the brothers, big Hub and little Bill, got in from the hunt they emptied their pockets. The pans held their winnings from the card games!

From that day on, I tried to pick my spots when big Hub or little Bill offered me money to do something for them!

As all young boys tried to do after being kissed, we wiped or rubbed the area. Hopeful it would lessen the jolt to our efforts to becoming a grown up!!

With money in our pockets and now knowing the content of those mysterious cloth covered pans, the three "Goobers," Tater, Dink, and Rabbit, left laughing. Chino growled at us as we left the back porch. He slobbered, belched, and then raised a leg and broke wind as he crawled into his doggie bed.

I ask Rabbit and Dink, "what are you guys going to do with your money?"

Rabbit mumbled something about the Ole Store and Dink laughed and then added he would like a Grape or an RC Cola, because it was hot. Not paying attention to what they said, Tater was daydreaming about that new baseball glove. He was saving his money to order from the Sears /Roebuck catalog.

Also, he was plotting a way to get Rabbit or Dink to pay for a cold drink for him. A true goober never pays for his drink if he works the scheme right!

Besides, those two would get to use the glove also, and the more I saved, the faster I would get to order the glove.

Thus begins the battle of wits and another story in the days of Three Goobers and a Nut.

How I Got My New Baseball Glove

The only thing stopping me from getting a new ball glove from the Sears Roebuck Catalog was having the money! I had been saving all I could find! I sure didn't want to work for it but money doesn't grow on the trees. At least that's what my brother told me! Maybe it sprouts from the ground, because I saw him burying his money in the dog pen and push the doghouse over that spot!

It didn't have a chance to grow much. I saw my sister watching him bury the money! I guess she didn't want the money to get wet! She must have heard him tell me he was saving for a rainy day!

She gave me a nickel not to tell my brother that she saved his money from getting wet. Then I made a dime off my brother by telling him who had his money! He knew it was gone because the doghouse had been moved and a big hole was in its place!

I now had one dollar and 15 cents. The glove was priced at nine dollars and 95 cents plus a shipping charge. That was a dollar and 70 cents and it came by mail. In the 60's there wasn't a UPS truck to deliver stuff! I needed ten dollars and fifty cents to pay for my dream glove. Every time I saw it in the catalog, I dreamed about the plays I could make on the baseball field.

The phone at my grandmother's house rang. She answered it and talked a few seconds before she said, "it's for you."

I was stunned! I almost dropped the phone as I placed it to my ear.

"Hello," I whispered and stuttered a second but louder, "hello!"

From the other end came a laugh! It was Aunt Dee Dee. She needed her lawn mowed. She wanted me to do the job for her. I froze. I couldn't talk. Some would say that was a miracle. Still others might call it a blessing for the silence! She being Uncle C's sister-in-law, he's my best uncle, meant I'd say yes.

When I answered yes she said, "I'll pay two dollars for each time you mow and 25 cents to help pay for gas."

I almost wet my pants! I'd have to ask my mom if I could use her gas mower. I asked Aunt Dee Dee, "May I call back after I talk to my mom?"

"Yes," she replied.

I hung the receiver in the cradle of the rotary phone, turned, and ran all over my mom! She had been listening to me talk to Aunt Dee Dee. She was always a step or two a head of me, or so it seemed. I got excited trying to tell her about the lawn-mowing job. Leaving out some of the details, I tried to convince Mom that I needed her gas-powered mower. I tried too hard to make my story believable. She turn away from me and shook her head Yes, but she added, "you'll have to push the mower to her house."

I called Aunt Dee Dee and gave her the good news, I could take the job.

"May I ask a favor of you?" I blurted out.

There was a few seconds of silence and then she said, "What is it Tater?"

"Well, you know how much I love to play baseball!"

"Yes," she replied. "My husband and sons were very good players in high school and later in the military service," she told me. "I'll show you some gloves and some pictures when you come to mow!"

Her reply almost made me forget my question!

"What was it you wanted as a favor?" she asked.

Calling all the strength a "goober" could gather I

blurted out, "will you loan me Ten dollars and fifty cents? I'll mow until it's all paid back! Let me explain," I pleaded.

But she told me to come on to her yard and we would talk then! She hung up!

I gathered my equipment to take to Aunt Dee Dee's yard. I grumbled that I wouldn't be able to order the glove until about the middle of July if I didn't get the favor I was about to ask of her!

I pushed the mower out of our yard. I crossed the dirt road into Aunt Fannie's yard and hit the trail towards Uncle Pete and Granny C's house; that's Rabbit's grandparents. I crossed their yard and went into Tipsy Ole Boots' woods, just across the road from the Old White Church building. Maybe I wasn't having a good day and it was fixing to get worse.

My luck was going down hill like a truck without brakes! Everything seemed fine as I walked and pushed the mower toward Aunt Dee Dee's yard. When I tripped and landed face first in a pile of moss. The moss was very damp and slick. I slid several feet on the moss. My clothes were soaked. I sat up and slung my muddy arms in disgust. The pictures of what I would do to the ones who did this, this wonderful prank, made my head throb!

Imagine me the lead "goober" being the butt of a prank!!!

I sprang to my feet looking for my mower and gas can. I saw a reflection of something to my left. It was two double cola drink bottles. Then it hit me those two goobers, Dink and Rabbit, got me again! There were pieces of wax paper that had held, I'd bet all the tea in Tibet, a couple of cheese and baloney sandwiches. I'll get those two!

I picked up my gas can and the two coke bottles, that was 4 cents towards my new glove. I found the wire that tripped me. I looped the wire around the neck of each bottle and hung them in a bush. I would get them on the way home. Bottles were worth two cents each at Old Tom's store at the crossroads.

I tried to get everything sorted out about what had just happened. How would I get Dink and Rabbit? But, seeing the mower changed my thoughts to the ball glove and the grass-cutting job ahead.

I pushed the mower toward the old barn on the land of Tipsy old Boots' brother. Their family home was separated from the barn by a row of apple trees and a row of plum trees. I was thinking about picking a plum or two when I passed by the barn. I checked to see if Tipsy Ole Boots was sitting on the porch, He usually sat on the front porch after his trip to Ole Tom's store for a Coca-cola and a baloney and cheese sandwich. I saw his dog but not him. Old Boots stepped out of the first stall of the barn and said, "You can have all the plums you can eat."

I let out a yell; I don't know what it was I said, but he asked if my momma let me use those kinds of words at home.

Catching my breath and trying not to wet myself, I thanked him.

As I passed under the plum trees, I picked as many as I could. I stuffed my pockets and pushed on to the mowing job. He got into his truck and headed toward his house in the curve.

I got to Aunt Dee Dee's hoping to get started before she saw the mud on my clothes. She met me as I pushed the mower into her driveway.

She directed me to the back porch.

"Take 'em off," as she handed a huge towel to me. "Use the hose to wash the mud off."

I pulled my jeans and shirt off and wrapped the huge towel around my chest. It was fresh smelling and warm from hanging on the clothesline!

She came back with a pair of cut off blue jeans and a football jersey. How she had my size clothes

THREE GOOBERS AND A NUT

was a mystery. Then I remembered her grandsons, Dink's cousins from Tennessee, often spent some time with her.

"Now get to mowin'," she fussed in her best southern drawl, trying to sound mad, but I knew better!!

After about 45 minutes of mowing, she began waving a dishtowel and motioning for me to stop.

On the patio table was cold lemonade and a plate of cookies, homemade and fresh baked!! I'll say it now, I would have mowed just for the cookies and lemonade!

She had the same qualities as my grandmother, soft spoken, but stern; Smelled like fresh baked pies, cakes, or cornbread, and she was always there with a HUG!

I figured now was the time to try to work a deal with her.

As I spun my story of the need for a new ball glove, she hummed a song and rocked her chair. She sat up and said "back to work."

"How much do you have to pay for that glove?" She asked.

I shouted, "eleven dollars and 65 cents," as I yanked the pull cord on the mower.

I pushed the mower across the grass underneath

the cross vine tree. The smell of cut up grass is a lot like a fresh cut watermelon.

Around the old barn, follow the fence that divided Ollie Bay's yard from Aunt Dee Dee's garden and I'd be finished mowing. Then I could offer her my "pay in advance" idea.

She was sitting on the back porch. I sat down.

Before I could ask, she handed me a ten-dollar bill and four half dollar coins! I was again lost for words.

"Here you look at these, while I get the lemonade," she said.

As I leafed through the many photos, she told a story with each one. She recalled all the names of each one in the photos and where they were taken. Each one brought smiles. One had her husband (William) in a gray uniform and Army was on the front of the shirt. He had played outfield on a team in the service. He had passed away several years ago. There were three living sons, P.J., Vern, and Soapy. All were good athletes. Soapy was the most gifted of the three. He had played football and basketball for Jacksonville State. It was right before me in the pictures she had.

She wiped her eyes and told me I had better catch all the balls hit at me.

With the deal made, she handed me my clothes and showed me the new shower her family had installed for her.

"Wash both ears" she advised.

Imagine that, she had me take a shower before she would let me go home. Plus, she had washed and dried my muddy clothes, made cookies, then loaned me the money for my new glove!!! Well, she really just paid for her lawn to be mowed all summer.

It was if I had another grandmother!

I started toward home, pushing the mower and patting my pocket to make sure my money was still there.

A loud yell echoed from behind me.

It was Ollie Bay. He was going to Ole Tom's store for his mom, Gem.

I couldn't wait for him to get to me. I was busting at the seams to share my good news!

As we walked, I remembered the coke bottles I founding the woods.

I asked Ollie, "do you have any schemes to get even with Rabbit and Dink?"

We turned to the trail in the woods at Tipsy Ole Boots barn. I showed Ollie Bay where the wire tripped me.

"Let's add a wire" Ollie said. "One there at that huckleberry bush and another down near the moss rocks."

"That will have to wait awhile," replied Tater. Grabbing the two bottles, Tater headed down the trail to order his ball glove!

Ollie Bay asked Tater, "what kind of glove are you going to order?"

"You'll never guess, never in a 100 years," crowed Tater.

Ollie answered "probably a darned old Yankee's glove" as he poked me in the ribs. He knew I love Mickey Mantle, the great centerfielder for New York, and I knew he was a dyed in the wool Detroit Tigers fan.

Out of the woods into Granny and Uncle Pete's yard, Ollie went right on the trail, by Cora Bell and Deck's plum trees, then to the dirt road to Ole Tom's store. I went toward Aunt Fannie's house.

For the first time in my life, I wasn't thinking about a prank to use on her. I was headed to the house to get Mom to order that Al Kaline, the right fielder of Detroit and favorite player of Ollie Bay, model 10687R six fingered, baseball glove.

Ollie and I yelled back and forth about the glove. He yelled he'd be glad when the glove got here. That would mean he didn't have to loan his glove to me during our games.

I returned, "I would have a surprise for him, Rabbit, and Dink; just wait two or three weeks!"

That's how long the catalog advised for the order from Sears to arrive!

This was Friday. As I flipped the pages of the catalog, I tried to pinpoint the exact day of the glove's arrival. Mother hasn't even filled out the order page. Plus, the check can't be sent until she puts my mowing money in the bank. Then there's the mailman, he's the slowest moving object of all time.

He gets to Ole Tom's Store about 11A.M. everyday. What does he do? Sits down at the counter next to the coke machine and shoots the bull with Big Barn, and Tipsy Ole Boots. WW II stories and the local gossip are not as important as my ball glove!

What could I do to get him back on his route and get my mail order on its way?

I needed a break. I slipped a half dollar into my pocket and scurried out the back door. I headed for Ole Tom's store. I left my remaining money in a pint jar, hidden behind the cans of vegetables in the can closet!

Maybe Ollie Bay is still at the store! I smell a baloney and hoop cheese sandwich with a double cola meal about to happen!

Then it hit me why Mr. O., the mailman, enjoyed his stop at the Ole Store. This was his break and relaxing period from his job.

If you live long enough and learn a lesson, from everyday life, it will prevent you from looking dumb at some point in life. Even the mailman has to STOP and smell the Roses of life!

It was my turn to stop and smell the—uh roses! (baloney and cheese)

I entered Ole Tom's store from the side door. Located by the door was a huge metal double sink. Every one washed their hands before having a sandwich or pork 'n' beans and crackers. It was a lunchtime thing with us kids, to wash like the grown ups and then buy our food from the store!

I got the mop bucket and turned it upside down on the floor. Standing on the bucket made me tall enough to reach the water faucet handles. I washed my hands then put the bucket back in its place. I wandered to the front of the store. There sat the mailman, Ole Tom, Big Barn, Big Hub, Little Bill, and Uncle Pete on the store porch.

Ollie Bay was sitting on the floor of the porch

with his feet and legs hanging over the edge. He had an RC cola and a moon pie. Looked to me as if he was enjoying both!

I raised the lid of the cold drink box, removed a Grape cola and, using the cap remover, popped the cap off. Ole Tom's wife, Hay-zella stood up. She was asleep behind the huge cash register; The same one that had been with the store forever. As she pushed a button and cranked the arm, bells dinged and a draw opened.

"That will be a nickel," she said as she leaned on the counter.

"Will you fix me a baloney and hoop cheese sandwich with mayonnaise, please?" I asked.

"You know that will be fifteen cents for the sandwich," she said, as if to say "can you pay for these things?"

I showed her the 50-cent piece. She almost leaped over the counter. She had the sandwich made in record time. I gave her the money and waited for my change. She rang up the amount plus the tax. I checked my change, 29 cents and took my food outside to sit with Ollie Bay.

I needed to pay Dink and Rabbit back for my fall in the woods that day! We ate and drank, laughing at nonsense as we discussed what to do to those two goobers!

The mailman drew my attention, as he stood up to tell those on the porch he had to go back to work. He called me to his car. He lifted a few sale papers and pointed to a huge box addressed to my family. It was too large to have just a ball glove, besides I hadn't give mom the money I had made today! I shrugged my shoulders, and with a somewhat smug attitude, walked back to the store porch. I told Ollie Bay about the box. He mentioned my dad had probably ordered some tools for his carpenter's job.

He asked me if I was paying attention to what was said when dad was building the frame for the shower stall on our back porch.

Of course not, when did I ever listen to anything that made sense? That was when dad told mom he needed some sort of tool to do a certain task. Sears Roebuck had the tool and he told her to order it for him.

We finished our drinks. I leaned over close to the screen doors of the store and burped really loud and gross sounding. Hay-zella was asleep, my little noise scared her, and she screamed and jumped up from her chair. She had some green beans in her lap, which went all over the store when she stood up! She yelled at us as we ran toward the old grain mill to hide!

Ollie Bay ran by instinct. If you are with or around Tater and some kind of blood curdling yell is heard, you better run or have a letter from the president! I ran because I was the guilty party!

We played on the cob pile behind the mill for a while, hoping that Hay-zella hadn't called my house to talk to mom. We crossed the branch at the rocks that we used to dam up the branch to make a "goobers" swimming hole! A few yards walking and we were at the Big Yard, famous for the best ball games ever!

I began to clean the gas mower. Mom didn't want the mower deck to start rusting, so after each yard mowing I had to clean the grass from the under carriage. Since I had mowed Aunt Dee Dee's yard in the early morning, the grass was still damp from the dew on the grass. Grass stuck to the mower deck like glue and when it dried it was very difficult to remove! I went to the tool shack for a long flat pry bar to scrape the dried grass off the mower deck.

I came out of the shed and there was the mailman in our yard. He was carrying the same box he had shown me at the store. I ran to open the screen door for him. He set the box on the table. Ollie Bay looked at me, then at the box, as if to say well, are you going to open it? I shook by head No!

I knew that if I messed with the box and something was misplaced, I'd get a leather belt across my backside. But, that didn't keep me from shaking the box! Shaking the box made no sound, but it was heavy!

We went back to my chore, cleaning the lawn mower deck. Ollie Bay was ribbing me about being afraid to open the package. I have to admit I wanted to, oh what the heck; I'll get a butt busting or worse, I could get grounded.

Mr. O was back on his mail route. I could make a good story that it came open when it fell as he put it on the mailboxes. Ours and Aunt Rosie Lea's boxes were side by side. The space between the boxes was ideal to wedge a package that wouldn't fit IN the mailbox! So it might have fallen off the mailboxes, well it sounded good at the time!

I slid the box to the middle of the kitchen table. Using a steak knife, I cut the wrapping tape on each end and slit the middle band next. Wadded up newspaper surrounded the content. I took each piece, from the box, as if it would break upon touch.

I could feel the nerves making the hair on my arms stand up! Ollie Bay got closer to the package trying to see what I uncovered as I removed the paper wads.

Two more layers of packing material removed and there was a box big enough to hold a glove! But, it was the wiggling pin stabilizer and wobbling shaft holder dad needed when he built our outdoor shower on the edge of the back porch. I removed that box. There was a dividing piece of cardboard. I lifted it from the box. Ollie Bay leaned over to look into the box. I had one eye closed and the other squinting in case what I was hoping for wasn't there!

"Its here" Ollie shouted.

I looked down into the box and there was my six-finger model 10687 glove. Ollie Bay picked it up. His jaw dropped open in total disbelief, as he read Al Kaline's name from the last finger of the glove. But, there was MORE to see in that box!

Mom knew we always need a ball. She had ordered three regulation baseballs for our games, plus the biggest surprise was the final box within the box. It contained a pair of baseball cleats. Man, I was floating on cloud nine!

Ollie Bay said, "see ya Tater!," as Old Bob, my bird dog, welcomed someone with a chorus of barking. I knew it wasn't good because it was a friendly bark coming from him!

Mom opened the screen door. I was caught like a

rat in a trap. My pal Ollie talked me into opening a package even though I knew better. Then he left me holding the BOX, uh, uh—I mean the bag!

Oh well, it all went by fast, my punishment that is. I had to pick two five-gallon buckets of green beans, take them to Old Hay-zella, apologize to her, and then help string the darn things!

Dog gone you Ollie Bay, half those beans should have been picked by you!!!

Brother Bill and the RA's

We were blessed in a lot of ways growing up.

An example was, Brother Bill, our preacher and youth director. He organized a church group called the Royal Ambassadors. He taught us that you never pay anyone back for something of value that is given to you. Instead you pass on in kind the deed to someone else in need!

We cut a load of firewood for an elderly man that summer. That way the wood was allowed to dry before he used it in the fall and winter. We took turns mowing the grass at the church. At home I got to baby sit, whether I wanted to or not! I guess home chores, such as watching my one-year-old niece, was pay back in kind when someone had to watch me!

One of the fun things we got, as a reward, was a

trip to the campsite of a friend of Brother Bill. It was on the Tennessee River at an area called South Salty.

The day of our RA camping trip started with a surprise, a trip to the Ole Store at the crossroads. Mother bought me a brand spanking new pair of blue jeans!

Cooter, my older sister, was packing my clothes for the trip. My job was to watch little Bell, my niece. Everyone said she looked like her grandmother Bell, so they nicknamed her Little Bell!

In the late 1950's there wasn't any type of disposable diapers, only cloth diapers. I guess Little Bell was tickled about me going to the river. So, she gave me a big send off, she wet her diaper and my new blue jeans! I let out a howl that any coyote would have enjoyed. I started crying and so did little Bell. My howl had scared her.

Cooter dashed into the room, scooped my niece out of my lap, and said, "what's wrong?"

Seeing the dripping's from the diaper, she burst out laughing.

I didn't see anything funny in the situation. So I cried even louder! Some how my sister got me under control, my jeans dry, and my clothes packed.

We met other groups from the surrounding churches and traveled to the campsite.

Our group had all the regulars: Willie Dee, Bernie, Ollie Bay, Little Hog, Billy Beaver, Strut, Foxhunter, and Tater. Dink and Rabbit, weren't old enough to go yet!

Other groups were there also which included: Farley, Mossy, B.C., Peck, Sam, Fats, Hugh the Pumpkin," J.B., John L., Tee Bird, Swifty, Buzzy D., Doc, Dolbert, Morgie, and Jam!

Most of the older guys from the other churches didn't stay over night. But those of us that stayed had the most fun, without being injured or worse, and lived to tell about it!

Bernie and Willie Dee built a fire for cooking wieners and burgers! Neither had every used a grill nor charcoal and especially lighter fluid!

The explosion left a couple of guys covered in soot and a lot of hair singed!

Both looked like Al Jolson, in makeup, ready to sing Mammy!

After the mess was cleaned up, a fire was built, (safely), from wood, and lunch was fixed.

After we ate, sleeping arrangements were made and tents pitched. Then a bell rang twice. This was the signal for us to go swimming in the Tennessee River! A first for many of us!

We raced to get into our swimming attire. Most of

the guys had cut off blue jeans. Others actually had swimming trunks!

The race to be the first one in the water almost drowned Farley. He was one of the first to the boat dock. He waited for the rest of us, but didn't see Fats rushing to do a cannonball dive! Fats bumped into Farley, knocking him into the water. Luckily, it was close to the ladder used to get out of the boats. I had heard Fats running thru the woods and had gotten out of his way. I had climbed down the ladder to the water. Farley when head first into the water and Fats went over him!

I guess the bump (Farley weigh all of 80 pounds and Fats, well he was over 250 pounds) knocked the breath out of Farley. Add the wave Fats caused when he hit the water, to the fact Farley swallowed half the river, one could imagine the results. But, fate put me in the right place and I got Farley by the hair on his head and pulled him to the boat ladder. Coughing and spitting river water, Farley held to the ladder until Hugh the Pumpkin and some of the older guys pulled him up on the dock.

After we got calmed down, the leaders showed us the proper way to dive. Then how to float, and how to bring a person to shallow water, even if they think they are about to drown! We learn a lot and had fun too!

Probably the most fun was Bernie hiding Willie D clothes. Willie D found some old newspapers in the boathouse and wrapped them around his waist. He tried to make it to his tent to get some clothes. Along the way, Bernie and the older guys set the papers on fire! Out of the paper and into the tent he dove, showing nature as he went!

He found his clothes and yelled "I'll get y'all for this!"

He did get back at Bernie by hiding his clothes at school during gym class that fall! Bernie's clothes were found in the girl's dressing room! To this day nobody knows how the clothes got there!!! Willie D just smiled and whistled as he walked away!

Knee-High Nighttime Baseball

We couldn't play ball some days because we were working in the fields. None of the ball fields close by had lights, so somebody had to come up with a way to play at night. Guess who? Yeah, it was Tater and his group of goobers! The goobers were the ones that Tater convinced to share the blame if his ideas went bust!!

My mom had three or four lights she would use to keep young animals warm. Especially the birddog pups my dad raised, trained, and sold! Baby pigs had to be taken away from the sow sometimes to keep her from laying down on them. So, naturally they needed warmth to survive. These lights were use for warmth to help them survive. But, the lights weren't used much in the summer.

I'd get the lights with the long cords. The further

the cords stretched from the house, the more area could be lit and our ball field grew in size for the night games!

Another item we borrowed was Gar-Gar's, (a grandchild's name for my dad), drop cords; Man, those 100-foot cords made a World Series possible. But, if I forgot to put them back where I got them, my pants would catch a dusting!

To get the ball field area covered light position was important. Those lights had clips so they could be fastened to objects. The lights had movable joints, attached to the clips, so the light could be directed to a spot. The first light went on the television antennae, which had to be climbed and the light and cord pulled up after I got on the roof! This light was behind home plate and pointed toward the pitcher's mound. Man, did my dad howl when the climbing of the pole caused the picture to fade!

If the light wouldn't stay in the position I wanted, I hauled a cement block up to the roof and laid it on the cord so it couldn't move. More howling about the roof; "if you cause a leak I'll skin your behind," yelled my Dad.

The next light went up on the telephone pole in right field. It held the line to the phone in Maw

Maw's house (my grandmother). Climbing that sucker, the pole, was tough but, I would use creative genius; Well, I always found an easier way to do a task to avoid as much work as possible. (I read a lot of Beetle Bailey comic books, also.)

Anyway, I sneaked my dad's spikes from his tool bag, strapped them on, up the pole, no problem! Then I used a hammer and nails to attach the outfield light to the pole. Rabbit and Dink would toss the end of the cord to me and I'd pull the light fixture up and put it in place.

The next light was at third base. The best place for this light was about twenty feet from the ground. Slight problem, how would I attach the light to the cable/wires (anchors), those that kept the power pole straight? It came to me like a flash of lightning, using the wooden ladder dad had built; it could be wedged against the wires and climbed up!

It's probably a good thing there were three "goobers" around to set up the ladder. It was very heavy. The stilts were twelve feet long and the base was three feet wide. The stilts were red oak and the steps were yellow pine, fresh and oozing very sticky rosin! The thing took five twelve-foot pieces of very heavy lumber! Carrying that monster felt like he used half of the logs in Granny C's woods!

THREE GOOBERS AND A NUT

Finally a bit of luck, the cables were in a parallel position, like (//). I put the grip clip on one cable and laid the light over the other. To keep the cord from putting pressure on the light fixture, I sent Dink into my house for freezer tape. It stuck well, was strong, and could be torn easier than my Dad's electrical tape!

"What about Aunt Bell?" asked Dink.

"Just get the tape, it's on top of the freezer" said Tater.

We had to hurry to get the tape back before she missed it. She got fussy about us wasting her tape.

The lights were up, now the field had to be laid out.

"We need an outfield fence," Dink and Rabbit stated.

"What are we going to use and where do we get it?"

Man these two are going to need a JSTK (jump-start tail kicking) I thought to myself. "What comes to your mind when you think fence?" I asked.

"The wooden sections of the flower bed borders at all the houses around the neighborhood" I said.

"It'll never work" Said Dink.

"Are you going to borrow or steal them?" asked Rabbit.

"We'll sort of borrow them." replied Tater.

"What does sort of borrow mean?" asked Ollie

Bay. He had just gotten back from Detroit, where he saw the Tigers play baseball.

"I smell trouble, you'll get us a tail busting, I know you too well." declared Ollie Bay.

"Not so loud it'll scare the "goobers" and they might not help get the fence." said Tater.

Most of the time I could get Ollie Bay to go along with my ideas. As we got older he out-thought me, a lot! The result was I would take all the blame! Dang it, we were supposed to share the blame, after all I was giving,——-shouldn't they receive?

My plan was for each of use to obtain six or eight sections of the flowerbed border fence from anywhere. Just remember where you got them. We would put them back later.

We made a list of houses with the border fence. Just about all houses had this type of fence. So, we decided not to take all from the same place.

The List: (each place has a kid or someone identified by a nickname)

Dink and Rabbit made their list, it included: Flip and Bee Bow's, Granny C's, Ole Tynch's Trailer, (those first three would not care, but these last two would go bonkers), Tipsy Ole Boots, and Showboat Hay-Zella!

Finally, a lesson sunk in, aggravate as many as

you can, life is too short and chances are few and far in between; so git 'er done, as the cable guy says!

Ollie Bay and I made our list, it included: Fox and Hound's house, my choice, because I was sweet on their sister, Suzy Q; the Pyramid of cans house, Ollie Bay's future wife lived there; the Two Fox Hunters, & Big Lu's house (they had Ole Chino, the original guard dog), because they loved sports and would put you up to any kind of mischief they thought was funny! The best part was how loud their sister could yell when she got mad at us for the mischief we created. She could cuss too, sailors blushed at some of the words she could say! I would have put Old Rocky, the mechanic, on our list, but he scared the bejebbers out of me when he raised his mechanical leg and it squealed. I could see him hiding and sneaking up behind me, then put those strong, greasy hands on my neck, and woe is me, I got to go to the bathroom!

That left Aunt Fannie, we couldn't leave her off the list. It was too much fun seeing her foam at the mouth, spitting and wiping snuff, and squawking about what we had done to her flowers and shrubs and that dang window.

I would have put Rosie Lea on the list, but it didn't bother her when I did things around her house. She would let me climb her fruit trees and eat all I wanted. I liked her cherry tree the most it was always loaded! And, her 17 year-old daughter's bedroom window was even with the limb I sat on to pick cherries!

We got the fence sections and no one ever said anything about their missing flower border fence. Mom couldn't figure how so many sections of the fence got into storage shed. She made a lot of friends smile when she gave them several sections of border fence that fall.

We used the sections to build a cool looking curved fence, just like the ones in Yankee Stadium or Tiger Stadium.

Still something was missing on our field. I saw it under the grape vines, a huge piece of net like material. It would make a great wall. Just like the one in right field, where the Dodgers played. (Ebbett's Field).

Cooter, my youngest sister, would think the idea was crazy, but I was going to hang that net in the tree for her. She loved "them Bums" from Brooklyn and the 1950's.

I had to climb two trees to hang that net, but man, the fun we had falling into the net making catches! Mantle, Aaron, or Snider would have been proud of us!

Ballgames require ground rules. This means, keep a fight from happening by following some set of rules. Our game rules were set, until the game started!

Under the propane gas tank was a double. If you dove into the net to make a catch and didn't field it clean, it was a triple. Over the net was a home run. If it went into the oak tree and stayed, it was a single, but if it came out, you could catch it for an out. If it hit the ground after falling from the tree it was a ground rule single! My house was like a backstop, but if a foul ball went on the roof and rolled off you could catch it for an out.

A small problem that made it difficult getting to a ball coming off the roof, was the shower stall on the back porch. It was at the corner of the house and you would have to run around it, to get to the ball coming off the roof. Plus, if the shower had been used there was water everywhere and it was always slippery. I might mention we didn't have indoor facilities yet! My brother, Butch, lived in the Old Veterans Apartments at college and he collected spare plumbing parts to repair problems in his apartment. My Dad took the parts and made an outdoor shower on the back porch and it drained directly into the yard!

Oh, if the outfielder could touch a section of fence he could stand up and dive over the fence, into the make believe "cheap seats," to rob a batter of a homerun!

We made rule as we played. You had to bat with both knees on the ground. You could run as far as third base, while standing, then get back down on your hands and knees and go home as best you could!!

The pitcher threw from his knees, then got up and fielded the ball. It was the same way for the other fielder, start on the knees, then stand, and run to the ball. Once the ball was fielded, you had to get back down to relay the ball to the other fielder. A fielder could go to any base, but had to be on his knees to catch the ball at that base. All runners had to slide! We would have broken every bone known to man if we didn't slide! Some got broken anyway.

Next came the ball, it was plastic, hollow, had many, many holes in its surface, and never went straight when thrown. By adding two strips of black electrician's tape, so that four sections were created, some of the holes were covered and weight was added.

As the air meets the ball, movement was quick or

difficult to hit; or it floated, straight making it easy to hit.

With what do you hit a plastic ball? A plastic bat is best but we managed to bust all of them quickly. We could use a regular wood bat but it busted (this is the late 50,s and early 60's no metal bats) the ball! So, we tried several things, a broom handle, (Aunt Fanny must of bought four or five brooms that summer), but they broke when they were swung against a tree; hoe handle, (not wise to cut Aunt Bell's garden hoe handle, she might use on us); shovel handle, (see hoe handle), all the wooden things used as a bat, busted the ball!

We managed to keep a supply of plastic balls. Finally, I came up with a solution for the bat problem. I had a collection of wooden bats. Most of them were broken. The men, who played independent baseball for the local teams, would give them away. They were the prize for recovering foul balls or a home run ball.

I would cut the broken part off and put a section of plastic pipe in its place. It was light for swinging, but didn't bust the ball.

Games lasted until we were exhausted, or we played nine innings. Sometimes we scored so much we'd play first team to 50 runs wins that game and start over. Who ever won batted last the next game! When the games ended, the guys had to go home.

Ollie Bay's house and Rabbit's grandmother's house were beyond the scary Old White Church. So, after the games we would walk or ride bicycles, the four of us, to their house, Ollie Bay's first. He lived about a mile away. Then we waked through the woods behind Ole Boot's house to Rabbit's grandmother's house. Rabbit stayed there a lot because it was three miles to his house. I loved Rabbit but not three miles worth after a night game.

After Granny chased Dink and me, trying to grab us by what ever, we left Rabbit and when back to my house. On the way, we passed by Aunt Fannie's, nothing beats a late night prank, so we took down her days washing from the clothesline. We fashioned a crude looking man and put it on the side porch. Then ran a garden hose thru the zipper of the pants and...Ran like our head was on fire and the flames were spreading!!!!!! We, or I, couldn't wait to tell Rabbit and Ollie Bay about the hose!

Dink said "I'm movin' to Texas 'cause I want to hide on the Indian reservation where my great uncle Cage Jarbour lives!"

Tired and hungry, we made it to my house. Dink would shower on the back porch while listening to WLS, a popular radio from Chicago. I made sandwiches for us. Mayo, green onion, baloney, and government program cheese on white bread! Plus, fresh cold cows milk, not pasteurized! Man would the expert on health flip about that diet!

We ate, I showered, then to the sound of crickets and a gentle wind blowing through the window screens, we fell asleep. Little did we know the topic of gossip, at the Ole Store, would be the man on Aunt Fannie's porch!

WHY IT'S BETTER TO BE SECOND, SOMETIMES!!

We were very lucky in lots of ways as we grew up in the 50's and 60's. However, we had a bit of bad luck, too! Maybe that's how the old saying "no good deed goes unpunished" came about!

Bill Beaver's dad was a huge baseball fan. He coached a team that Hog and Beaver played on and often he let us older guys play defense in practice.

Most of the time pickup games were played instead of practice. We had a field laid out in places where a game could be started at the drop of a bat, a glove, a ball, or a hat! Some of the places were: the sandy part of the old store parking lot, Ollie Bay and Bill the Beaver's Black Angus pasture, the playground behind Tenbroeck School, Dink's pasture, hand mowed to the shape of a diamond.

The curve in the outfield, where the short grass stopped and the tall grass began, was the boundary for a homerun at Dink's. Same as a fence only softer and not as high! Plus, Tee Tommy and Bee Bow's lot; and the most often used, Tater's Field of Dreams or Aunt Fannie's Nightmare. The name of the last two depends on whom you ask!

We would get to bat once or twice at the practice session. As usual, with the "Nuts" in our group there was always an argument about who was to be first to bat, play second base, pitch, or catch in the pickup games. The pickup games were more fun because we got to bat more times.

Beaver's dad had moved to Michigan to work in the Automobile factories. The companies give away tickets to Detroit games and he developed a love for the Detroit Tigers! Eventually the family moved back and began farming for a living.

There weren't a lot of extracurricular activities, but baseball had always been one! It didn't allow us to get into mischief as MUCH!!!

Naturally, the farm had a truck. It carried everything and everybody. The everybody being the community ball players, and everything being farm things; like plows, wrenches, bolts, and nuts, diesel fuel (in a hundred gallon storage tank)!

There were rags to wipe grease and oil spills away, to prevent dirt from collecting on the tractors. Dirt causes a lot of wear and tear on mechanical parts. Also, a huge can of hand cleanser to remove the diesel fuel from where ever it was on the body. If left on the skin long enough fuel causes the skin to blister, like a too long in the suntan. The baseball equipment was on the truck too. It was stored in an Old army duffle bag, bought at the unclaimed baggage store. (Remember the duffle bag for later)

The gang began to form at Ollie Bay's house on this particular day. A good day for a baseball game, because we numbered about 16 or 18 players. We ranged in age from about 11 to 16. Today would be a community game with very few pitches in a row without a discussion (argument).

Let's see if I can remember the names: Hog, Beaver, Hound and Fox (cousins of Hog) Rabbit, Dink, Tater (that's me), Ollie Bay, Trottin' Huey, K.T., Hands, Foxhunter, Tee Tommy and Bee Bow, Strut, Bubblegum, and VW!

We jumped the fence. Someone tossed the bag of equipment into the open pasture.

When the Bag hit the ground, the discussions began.

"I'm the catcher," yelled Dink.

THREE GOOBERS AND A NUT

"Naw, you ain't," retorted Beaver!

Being older got most of the choices of positions on the field.

"I've got first base!" yelled Foxhunter.

"I want second!" chirped Bee Bow.

Trottin' Huey chimed in with a menacing snarl, "I'll pitch!"

Having said that, the rush for the equipment bag started.

Hog grabbed the bag and ran toward the backstop that we had built. Nothing slows a baseball game like having to chase a loose ball. Some of the games we didn't have a catcher, so the batter had to pick up the ball and throw it back to the pitcher when he swung and missed thus the need for the backstop. It wasn't fancy. It just got the job done. The backstop was under the oak tree where all of the Black Angus lounged around, when they weren't grazing.

Beaver was yelling at Hog to drop the bag. Hog never broke stride, giggling at Uncle Beaver, zigging and zagging as he ran, to avoid getting caught. All the noise spooked the 20 or so cows. As they crashed into the woods and created a cloud of dust, the Beaver tackled Hog! Hog rolled into the ditch just behind the backstop. The equipment bag rolled to the backstop and Beaver, after three or four flips, landed on his feet and with a scowl on his face, crowed "gotcha Hoggy!" Hog was laughing so hard he lost his breath! How he rolled around under the tree and didn't land in any cow manure is beyond me!

Rabbit grabbed a bat and began swinging to loosen up.

He crowed, "first batter!"

Hog popped up, out of the dust, and ran to play shortstop. Tee Tommy settled in leftfield and the Hound when to centerfield. Hound's brother, the Fox played right field. Strut snagged practice throws at third base, while Bee Bow was inspecting Hog to see if he had any cow manure on his clothes or hands.

He said, "I don't want him to throw me something besides the ball!"

The woods echoed with laughter!

Tater, Dink, K.T., Hands, Bubblegum, VW, and Ollie Bay, joined Rabbit at the backstop. Beaver began putting the shin guards and chest protector in place before reaching for the mask!!

The mask was to protect the face from foul balls. No one had noticed that the duffle bag had absorbed diesel fuel from the bed of the farm truck and into the liner of the mask, also! In the confusion created by the creature scientifically identified as—Swineacus Hardnosia wantacauseafightcus or commonly called—Hog, dirt had gotten on the bag where the fuel had soaked into material of the bag and then into the Mask padding!!

The problem of being first was about to happen. Poor Beaver wore the mask first! Most of the fuel rubbed into his skin. He peeled, like an onion, one layer at a time. It took about 6 weeks to heal.

The pain didn't come about immediately. He tried to rub with a cloth, but that caused a lot of irritation and spread the fuel! If we had remembered the cleaner it might have lessened the strength of the fuel! Tee Tommy remarked that it was the first time he had seen a beaver skinned without a knife! We all laughed, but we also felt sorry for the Beaver!

Strut told Beaver that he would try the fuel treatment if it cured any of Beaver's pimples! But the whole pasture of ball players scattered when Rabbit began to flap his ear as he, Dink and the rest of the us sang, "Ring around the Rosies!"

Beaver when off like a bomb! Hollering and throwing anything he could find. Throwing at anybody he could see! Those rings of pain were not easy to forget.

The gang always took their shots at a victim if they made a mistake, but it was all in fun. We would have fought anyone for those in our group; although most of the time it was someone in the group we would fight.

Beaver was lucky the fuel didn't get into his eyes. Maybe that's what caused him to be an Optometrist instead of a Dermatologist!

FISHING ON THE BIG ROCK

It was late summer. All the fieldwork was slow. The cotton was beginning to pop open. Corn was turning brown, watermelons were overripe, and the cucumbers were just the right size to be used as footballs. We would do just about anything for entertainment!!!! Cucumber football!!

We had finished picking the last of the cucumbers from the garden for pickle making! When Willie Dee lobbed a huge ripe cucumber toward Tater and yelled, "catch!"

Tater reacted into a position to catch the vegetable! Not knowing that the cucumber was overripe and would splatter when touched, Tater put his hands out to catch a touchdown pass. Instead, he got a bubble bath in the aroma of rotten cucumber.

Willie snapped into action! To avoid being punished for the howling I was about to start and the cucumber I got hit with, he yelled, "let's go fishing at the Big Rock!"

Forget that I was covered in cucumber mess, I ran to get the fishing poles and a shovel to dig worms!

Auntie B had promised Dink a chance to go fishing with Willie D and me. This was to be an adventure, plus downright entertaining, and fun to boot!

She made us promise to watch Dink very close. She was afraid we would let him fall in the creek. Heck, he wouldn't have a chance to fall, we'd push him!!!

The fishing trip began with a buggy ride to Old Hoss' barn. Once we got there, I made a side trip to his watermelon patch, which was a necessary goober training procedure. Dink had to be shown that taking watermelon's on a fishing trip was a good goober's training ritual!! Plus, that's what the burlap sack in the old buggy was used for, carrying watermelons.

"Are we going to steal them?" asked Dink.

Here was another chance to pass on a step in the goober's training.

"NO! It ain't stealing if you promised to return them!"

"Plus something extra!" I said.

"How are we going to return them, if we eat the melons on the creek bank?" Dink asked.

"I'll show you later!" said Tater.

Man this goober was going to be tough to train, all those questions.

We took three medium size melons. Just big enough to take care of our appetite, but not so big we couldn't carry them. I put two in the sack and tied the top.

Dink had the sack slung over his shoulders like football pads. The watermelons weighed about five pounds each, a good strength builder for a young goober. I carried the other melon and Willie D was carrying the poles and a glass fruit jar full of big red worms!

We hit the trail that lead to the Big Rock, the secret fishing hole. Well, to us it was secret.

The trail was a worn down path, made by cows going to the woods.

There they found shade from the sun, and a patch of sweet smelling honeysuckle to munch on while cooling off during the day.

The path, bordered by black berry vines and red nose briars that have needle like spines that will snag any article of clothing.

Dink didn't like the trail, "cause them blarers are stickin' me!" he yelled.

The usual 10 to 15 minute walk would put us on the creek bank, but the goober trainee slowed everything down. Willie Dee teased Dink, "want me to throw you in the briar patch?"

"No! I want to go home!" said Dink.

Another lesson in the training of a goober, develop a tough hide. This was needed because we all get teased or harassed by some of our group!

We got to the Big Rock, a huge boulder that was about ten feet in diameter and stuck about 6 feet above the creeks water level. The top was worn in the right areas, so each person had a sort of seat. The rock made fishing easier. No limbs to hang our line, and someone had put rocks in a circle and had built a fire a day or so before we got there!

Little did we know the fire was going to be needed!

To get on the Big Rock you had to walk a huge tree trunk that had fallen beside the rock.

All little goobers think they can do anything an older goober, or old nut can do.

Wrong!!!

Willie D told the little goober to wait, he would come back and help him get to the rock.

Did the little goober listen?

Did John Kerry get elected?

Here goes Dink on to the log, trips /slips into the water.

I jump in—it's waist deep on me, and neck deep on Dink. I grab his shirt, pull, up pops Dink spitting water, screaming for help. Then Willie D's big hands grab my arm and Dink's leg dragging us on to the big rock!

Dink was crying and screaming when Willie Dee yelled, "Quiet! y'all are scaring the fish."

"Tater get some dry sticks," he said.

He built a fire, and pulled Dink's wet clothes off. He hung them near the fire to dry. Dink sat bundled in the burlap sack to stay dry and warm. As for me, I just sat close to the fire and dried. Willie D then lit his homemade pipe, pulled off his big shoe and sock, put his cane pole between his toes, put his hat over eyes and began to daydream.

While we fished and dried, Willie slit open the melons. Then he cut each half into pieces small enough to be held in one hand. That way we could eat and fish at the same time. Each bit of watermelon would have several seeds. We would then see who could spit a seed the longest distance.

We caught enough bluegill and shell crackers to

have a feast. It was time to go home, but before we left the creek we made Dink promise not to say anything about falling in the creek!! Before leaving we put the fire out. A safety lesson for the goober!!

Now I'd show Dink how to return the melons we borrowed. We put the rinds in the sack, added the remaining worms and dirt and feed them to the cows when we got to the herd. How were we to know cows don't fish!!! Anyway, the worms would help with the rinds.

We loaded the buggy and headed home. Aunt B's biscuits and gravy along with the fried fish tasted wonderful. Then we climbed the stairs to the pump house loft where we slept in the summer. If we were lucky, it would rain and rock us to sleep using the sound of rain hitting the tin roof as the music.

So, on goes the training of a goober; a never-ending chore!!!

THE WATERMELON PATCH

One of the best parts of farming for a living was the fun we had working in the fields. Uncle C grew anything that would sell for a profit. Plus, he had a lot of extra people to help, other than just our family. All the kids in our community were use to some kind of farm work because that's how and where we lived!! It was an unwritten rule that we work for the family we were visiting that day.

Like the watermelons and cantaloupes Uncle C would grow to sell at the Farmers Market in Chattanooga or at the crossroads on the weekends. All the goobers, and some of the Nuts, helped carry the fertilizer to the planters on the day we seeded the watermelon patch on Uncle H.L.'s farm. His land joined Uncle C's woods. Being married to sisters made renting land to a brother-in-law for cultivation rather easy! The difficult part was deciding which crop would produce the best yield and make the most money. We all hoped for a huge crop of melons to sell and maybe some big ones left over for a watermelon cuttin' (party)!

Uncle C had set the planters on the ends of the cultivator to plant the watermelon seeds in the smaller field of Uncle H.L.'s place. The reason was to give the plants lots of space to spread their runners or vines. Normal planters were set at 32 to 34 inches apart but for the watermelon seeds it was 48 inches between the rows. We were interested in having a lot of blooms to develop, for the bees to pollinate, and become huge watermelons or a mouth-watering cantaloupe, not how wide the rows had to be!

One of the enjoyable parts, there were a few times work could be fun, of planting season was getting a chance to drive an old truck that hauled the fertilizer and seed. I was too short to reach the pedals but the best improviser of all, Willie D, solved that problem. He attached wood blocks to the pedals making them easier for me to reach. I started the old Studebaker truck, pushed in the clutch, put the gear shifter into low gear and tried to let the clutch pedal out slowly. The idea was to not lurch and dump the stuff off the back of the truck. Working the clutch and the gas at the same time requires lot of practice. It's similar to patting your belly and rubbing your head at the same time or vice versa. You've got to practice! I got that practice in the fields and sometimes on the dirt roads between the fields and home. Anyway, I did fair this time. The fertilizer didn't fall off the truck, but I managed to dump Ollie Bay and Rabbit. Dink and Willie had been dumped before and knew to hang on tight! All that hollering caused me to stomp the brakes and bounce my head off the steering wheel. Starting over my next attempt to drive was a bit smoother than the first try! Everything was just fine until Willie D hollered for me to stop. Instead of pushing in the clutch and let the soft dirt slow the truck to a stop, I stomped the brake, the truck backfired and lurched forward. My head banged off the back of the truck cab! Dink, Rabbit, Ollie Bay, K.T. and Hands all tumbled off the bed of the truck. Willie D had tried to remain cool and calm, but he exploded when he rolled, head first, off the truck bed and crumpled his new straw hat. He had just traded a dozen eggs, plus a game rooster and a settin' hen, to the rollin' peddler for that hat!

The peddler had an old school bus loaded with store type items and traveled by the people's farms. This gave the women of the farms a chance to get certain goods without taking time out of the workday to, as we used to say, "go to town."

Aunt B saved me from a thrashing from Willie D. He had gotten into her eggs that she usually put with her churned butter to trade for sugar and cocoa mix. I warned him that I'd tell her who took her eggs and the hen too! That slowed him down but he was still hot under the collar. All the "goobers" were laughing at him with his hat jammed down to his ears and his eye peering out from under the hat brim! It reminded me of a turtle looking out of its shell. He wouldn't let me drive for along time. So he got even with me that way!

About three or four weeks after the planting, we would have to hoe the watermelon patch! That meant a suntan, and blisters on your hands if you forgot your field gloves. A wooden hoe handle can rub a blister in a heartbeat and if sweat got into the wound, it caused a lot of pain. Hoeing the field was to remove as many weeds as possible. Watermelons and cantaloupes need all the rainwater they can get and weeds steal water if allowed to grow uncontrolled. After the weeding, by the hoe, we would go back and uproot as many tall growing weeds as we could by hand. Then we kept check on the number of days needed to grow the melons and cantaloupes. Usually about 80 to 85 days from the planting day meant a ripe product. In the next 21days some Nitrogen had to be spread around the plants to help them grow faster and bigger, if we got rain. The cultivator, used to spread the nitrogen (soda) had one hopper mounted in the middle to distribute the nitrogen pellets. It was twice as big as the fertilize hoppers used to plant the seeds. If we got the good showers (rain), the vines grew so fast that they crossed the plowing lanes and the soda had to be hand spread. Other wise the tractor tires would smash the vines.

It sounds simple enough for us to get a delicious treat from all that work.

Not so fast, y'all! To quote Tom Hanks, "Houston, we have a slight problem".

Of course, our problem was on earth. Our problem was human more than technical. As we worked the field of watermelons toward being sold at the Farmers Market, we encountered those good ole boys called "melon stealers". Lose a bunch of your best melons and there goes the profit we had worked for all spring and summer. No one wants to pay top price for a second or third-rate product. So, we had to come up with a way to scare off these scavengers. A scarecrow might be able to work on the varmints, crows, raccoons, even a fox or coyote. But we had to work wonders to prevent those "good ole boys" from raiding our melon patch before we pick the best one's to sell at the farmers market! The remaining watermelons are there for the picking to anyone who would come by Uncle C's and ask for them.

Dink, and his nephew K.T., spent almost a month guarding the melon patch at night. Some nights there were just skeeters and gnats to scare off. Other nights there were four legged varmints that craved our melons. But, the two-legged varmints were the most trouble. They were a hardheaded bunch. So, to make 'em believers of the idea we were not going to let them steal the best watermelons we had, a trap was set.

The night before we were to take a load of watermelons to the big farmers market in Chattanooga, K.T., Dink, and Rabbit camped out behind the feed bins in the pasture. They were across the dirt road from the watermelon patch when a car slowly made its way along the road. Dink, Rabbit, and K.T. knelt behind the feeders and waited. The car went past the melon patch but turned around below Dink's house. The sky was very bright. A full moon showered the area with enough light a blind man could almost feel it! Suddenly the lights went out! Slowly the car came back up toward the melon field. The car stopped in front of the feed bins, four doors opened and 4 boys got out, leaving the doors open! The first foot that landed in the melon patch was greeted by the blast of a 12 gauge shot gun!

One of the members of the car yelled "Hey, we're having car trouble"!

The replied was a second shot from a 20 gauge gun and the advice, "Get back in your car and go have it some were else, this station is closed!"

In rapid-fire order 1,2,3,4, doors slammed, an engine started, wheels spun into the dirt. Dust rose and rocks flew, and cuss words rang from all inside the car as it went into the night.

The next morning we found empty and several full cans of their beverage in the ditch.

We knew who was after the watermelons, because "Biggun" (nickname derived from the fact he was the bigger of a set of twins) (his name was J.T.), his little brother, Peety (his name was J.P.), Doc, a drinking buddy, and Long Distance (because he was 6'11") had helped hoe and weed the patch. They were going to load up some good size melons and sell them to a grocery store for some quick money.

The next two days were hot and long! First, we scattered a couple of bales of hay in the small trailers (8ft by 10ft). The hay was to keep the watermelons from bruising while we loaded and unloaded them. We made paths for the tractor and trailer by moving the vines and smaller melons to one side or the other as the tractors were driven into the field. Uncle C and Willie D would point out the best melons. Using their pocketknives they cut the stem being sure to leave about 2 inches attached to the watermelon. Uncle C told us that way the watermelon would leak! *It's the truth!* Try it by pulling the stem completely out of the watermelon then wait about thirty minutes and the sap will ooze out of place where the stem was attached.

They pointed, we carried them to a spot and made a pile. When the tractor got to that spot, it was easier to load the trailer and not walk yourself to exhaustion carrying watermelons across a 4 or 5-acre field. The system worked well. As one trailer left the patch with a load, the other trailer (4ft by

8ft) would make a trip into the field being pulled by Ole Red. His wagon was rigged with a tongue that could be attached to the draw bar of the tractor and pulled wherever!

That's one to think about if it's pulled by a tractor it's called a trailer, but if a horse pulled it we called it a wagon!

Me, Ollie Bay, Willie D, and Bernie picked, toted, and loaded the wagons with melons. The four night owls, who had attempted to pick a few watermelons the other night, never came to help! Dink, Hands (Dinks other nephew) and K.T. worked in the shade loading the big truck and discussing the fun they had the night before. Hands came to Aunt B's from his other grandmother's home near Skirum. Hands was disappointed that he wasn't there for the fireworks.

Sometimes we would sweat so much a melon would slip out of our grasp. Oops, a busted melon, but not to worry it was soon eaten, and before Uncle C had seen the rind which was tossed in the woods or high weeds. Dink and the loading crew could cut their melon instead of intentionally or accidentally dropping at least one melon then feed the rinds to the cows! Uncle C was in the field with us pickers most of the time so Dink's crew could goof off some of the time! Staying busy while working for Uncle C was serious business. He expected a 12-hour workday for the 8 hours he was willing to pay us.

We loaded about a 200 watermelons and maybe 100 cantaloupes in the big cattle truck then put two long bales of straw hay between the melons and the end gates. The hay kept the produce from rolling into the gates and also gave us a place to sit or sleep on during the trip to the market. Also we picked about 20 dozen (240 ears) of yellow sweet corn to sell.

There would be 7 people going to the market the next day, each had to be fed and watered. We couldn't eat at a café, too expensive! So, we helped Aunt B put together brown bag meals that were better tasting than any café food! We had 3 dozen fluffy, big as your fist size biscuits, churned butter in a wide mouth (to get your hand inside to dip the last bit of butter out) quart fruit jar, a pint of grape jelly and a pint of strawberry jam, a 10 gallon wooden barrel filled with tea, a bag of home made jerky and 7 dozen home made sugar cookies, or as we called them tea cakes! Plus, a number of cantaloupes and watermelons we didn't sell. No chance of going hungry! Maybe there would be some of the corn left. Fresh-shucked corn is a treat,

THREE GOOBERS AND A NUT

especially when salted and Ole Dink remembered to take a jar of salt! That "goober" is beginning to catch on as to how things get done. He even took a small nail and put a few holes in the lid to sprinkle the salt!

Time for bed! We would sleep in the loft of the shed out back. It has always been called the "pump house." At one time the main source of water came from the well inside the cinder block room that also stored the canned goods made each year. All the goobers and nuts sleep there! There had to be 6 or 8 mattresses stacked in one corner, plus a set of bunk beds in another corner with mattress and springs for each bed. The room was huge! Maybe 16 ft wide and 32 feet long and a TIN roof! On a rainy night sleeping was great. Listening to each drop hit the roof would be like having someone rock you to sleep.

Uncle C was leaving at 3 a.m. The trip was about 85 miles. We would follow AL Hwy 75 to Davis, GA. off Sand Mountain by the winding Georgia road that had 6 or 7 hairpin turns, Uncle C usually pulled into the gas station about the third turn. He filled the trucks tank with gas and we filled the restroom with all the gas us goobers could muster. He sold 10 watermelons, 10 cantaloupes, and 4 dozen ears of corn while we were there!

We crawled back into the bed of the truck. We thought about sleeping again but at the bottom of the mountain we made another stop at a store just like Ole Tom's Store. Uncle C had us unload 5 dozen ears of corn, 20 watermelons and 20 cantaloupes. He handed me a pencil and a small wire bound notebook. He then told me to write down what he had sold at the two stores. We made 7 more stops as we traveled up US Hwy 11 toward Chattanooga. The load got lighter and the space in the back of the truck got larger with each stop.

One of the stops was a store that was also the post office of Wildwood, Georgia. All those goobers woke up when the truck hit a pothole, as Uncle C pulled in beside the store, rattling everybody and everything in the bed of the truck.

Rubbing my eyes and trying to get awake I heard him say, "feed those boys" to Willie D.

"Come with me Tater," he said.

I'd eat later with Uncle C.

We stepped into the store where the owner sat sipping coffee. He shook Uncle C's hand. I looked outside at Willie D and those 4 goobers stuffing butter and jelly into those fluffy biscuits.

I snapped to attention when Uncle C asked "How many watermelons are in the truck?"

THREE GOOBERS AND A NUT

"Seventy-five," I said.

The man said "Take 'em ALL, but they have to be put in my spring water by that water oak tree down in the grove. Its got the white X painted on it."

Uncle C said, "sold, and I'll give you what ever cantaloupes I have on the truck. Let us eat a biscuit and we'll unload them."

Before I could move the owner took my arm and whispered to me, "you get 5 cents for each melon not busted or a crack in the rind! Don't tell anyone! Just make sure none are damaged. See me later."

We ate the biscuits and jelly, and then unloaded the truck. They thought I had gone crazy. I ran my hand over ever melon as it was put in the spring.

I told them, "just saying good bye."

The number of melons was 78. There were 7 damaged. We could eat those on the way back to Tenbroeck, Alabama.

I went inside the store. He ask, "how many?" I told him "78."

He looked puzzled.

"Don't ask or it will...never mind!" I said.

He handed me four dollars. "That's too much money!" I said.

He said, "you earned it. I was watching you rubbing the melons as they were put in the spring!"

"Let me have this old metal bucket and some chunks of ice from the old ice house out back." I asked.

You must be crazy, but he said "OK" as he scratched his head!

I removed 7 RC cola drinks from the wooden crate. I put the drinks in the old bucket. I handed him a dollar, but he wouldn't take it.

"The drinks are on me." he said.

I shook his hand and said, "Thanks."

I got some pieces of ice, put them in with drinks, covered the bucket with a box lid and set the bucket in the truck bed. I climbed in and sat on the bucket.

K.T., Dink, Hands, and Rabbit were up next to the cab of the truck asleep. Dink sat up and point to the bucket. I motioned for him to be QUIET!

"Come over here." I whispered.

Then I began to tell Dink about the deal I swung with the storeowner and what was in the bucket.

"You get the truck stopped at the old picnic table pull off at the Alabama State Line and I'll do the rest." I whispered to him.

We headed back toward home. No need to go to the Farmers Market because Uncle C had made friends with the storeowners from past trips of selling his farm products. Today he sold everything before we got to the Tennessee state line!

Dink got Willie D's attention by telling him he had to GO NOW! We pulled off at the state line bus stop! Seems like everybody needed to go because the truck was empty except for me!

Uncle C came to the back of the truck. I stood up, removed the box lid I was sitting on and pulled an ice-cold RC cola out of the bucket and handed it to him.

"Where did you get this?" He said.

"Don't worry, I didn't steal them!" I told him.

"How many have you got?" Was his next question, but before I answered, I put a suggestion to him, "we've worked hard for you the past week. How about a little reward for the gang? I'll get the drinks, we've got those teacakes Aunt B made, and if you'll buy everyone a Cheeseburger it'll be an old fashion picnic. You just sold over 200 watermelons, 100 cantaloupes and I don't know how much garden corn!"

He looked at me smiled thru his false teeth, and said "Yeah, I will do it, but you've got to tell me how you got the drinks without money, I ain't paid anybody yet."

As we walked to the order window I spun my story. We got our food and walked to the truck. Such grumbling from the goobers, "Shame on y'all," I teased.

We spread the sandwiches on the picnic table and I brought the old rusty bucket off the truck and produced an ice-cold bottle of RC for the dirtiest and tiredest melon sellers on Sand Mountain. The questions stopped and laughter began...between bites of food that is!

Willie D talked Uncle C into letting him drive home which was around 50 miles.

I wanted to see that shower stall on the back porch at my house. I was beginning to smell like Pepe La pew, the skunk! This was one time no one had to tell me to bathe.

This had been a long trip but it made us aware that earning a living wasn't always the easiest thing to do. Never mind how hard I tried to find an easy way out of work. I usually had to work twice as long to do half as much work before I finished the job anyway! Beetle Bailey where were you when I needed you? If I could see the forest instead of the trees maybe I wouldn't get into so much trouble and mischief!!!!!

Don't Go Bird Huntin' If You Can't Shoot

In 1940 or 1941 my Dad bought a Remington 1148 Sportsman shotgun. In that period of the century money was not spent for unnecessary things. If it didn't provide something useful, food, clothing, transportation, or shelter, most folks would consider it to be a waste or mismanagement of money! Many a trail of gossip could be grown with a vivid imagination as to the way other folks spent their money. My Dad worked at the Army Depot during the period of WW II. Thru the week, he lived on base. On the weekend, he came to Tenbroeck where Mom, Cooter, (my sister), and Butch, (my brother) were living, with my Maw Maw and Paw Paw G.

During that span of time, Paw Paw G purchased

20 acres behind J.B.R's General Store. Pawpaw cleared the land and built a house. Uncle C bought land about a mile from there and after helping build Paw Paw's house, he and Aunt B started their house. Then mom started framing our house with Paw Paw G's help. We lived maybe 200 feet from Maw Maw G.

Besides my family, there were mom's two older sisters, both married with 5 kids between them, plus a younger brother, J and a younger sister, Little Bob, all under one roof!

All this is a brief attempt to paint a picture of the need of a gun. Not to shoot people, but to provide food. Some food was grown. No large chain of food stores with shelves stocked with items to be purchased. The hunting provided meat for the table.

The house Aunt B and Uncle C were renting burned! Nothing was saved! So they moved in with Maw Maw G.

Aunt D's husband was overseas fighting for all of us! Not having enough money to pay rent and buy food she came home to Tenbroeck, too! My family was in the same situation, not enough money to pay rent and buy food close to dad's job.

Uncle C farmed for a living. All members of the

families got to do their share of farm work, like milking and feeding the cattle, gathering eggs and slopping the hogs! Tending the garden, gathering field corn, and yes we picked COTTON!! We got to do other things besides work. We fished and best of all we hunted! Any hunting trip was a fun trip and the thought of food coming from the wild was special! I can still taste the fried quail and hot biscuits with sawmill gravy, that Aunt B, mom or Maw Maw G fixed after the bird hunts, now!

Until Dad ordered his gun, the 20-gauge model 1148, Dad and Uncle C shared a single shot bolt-action 12 gauge shot gun. That made it tough to kill more than 1 quail on a covey rise. So, he ordered a gun just like Uncle C's. When those two when hunting the birds, a feast fit for a kings table would be enjoyed.

Uncle Jay hunted snapping turtles! He used a stiff wire that had a huge barbed fishhook attached to the end. He hunted the branches and creeks, looking for a turtle's den. He would poke the wire in the den and if there was a turtle in the den it usually snapped at the hook. If the turtle latched on to the hook or if it stuck into the turtle's shell, a battle began. A tug of war was about to take place. I would tag along to carry the burlap sack used to carry the turtle back home. There are 7 different tastes in the meat of the turtle according to legends of old hunters. He had a second wire with a razor blade attached to the end. Just in case we surprised a snake or it surprised us! I've seen many a snake lose his head striking at Uncle Jay's razor blade.

I only went turtle hunting because I could play in the water. But, I sure enjoyed the soup Maw Maw G made using the meat of the turtle.

Until I was 13 years old, my BB gun was all I had ever shot. Dad let me handle the 20 gauge, but not shoot it. I was shown the safety button and how to load the gun. I was unaware of the recoil if not held tight on the shoulder.

I got one of my hair-brained ideas. I'd go hunting! No one here to stop me!

I took Old Bob, our liver spotted retriever, my dad's gun and his hunting vest, and headed for the cornfield next to Booger Hollow. There were plenty of quail there. I was craving fried quail, hot biscuits and sawmill gravy for supper that night.

Old Bob struck a hot trail about 100 feet off the dirt road. He sniffed, wagged his tail one or two times and then went motionless. I eased toward the spot I though the covey would be, kicking the weeds and brush pile. That was supposed to make the birds fly or as it's called a "covey rise". They did! The rush of excitement, of my first covey rise by myself, caused me to forget to hold the stock of the gun tight against my shoulder. As I aimed the loosely held shotgun and pulled the trigger, the recoil of the shot fired, was more than I could handle. The gunstock slapped my jaw and nose! Blood flew from my busted nose and lips. I stumbled to a tree and sat the gun down. Bleeding and hurting all over, I pressed a hand rag to my mouth and nose to slow the flow of blood. It was the cleaning rag for the gun. Dad had it in his vest. He always wiped the gun clean after each hunt.

As I sat against the tree, trying to remember what had happened, there sat Old Bob in front of me. Lying at his feet were two quail! I patted his side and rubbed his head. I guess my shot had hit both on the covey rise. He had what looked like a smile on his face. Somewhat of a look like I told you to be careful but you didn't listen! That dog was smarter than lots of folks, especially me!

I put the two birds in the hunting vest and began the walk back to the house. It was a mile or more following the road. About half as far if I cut through the field and woods near Uncle Pete and Granny C's house.

As I passed their house, Granny C was sitting on her porch. When she saw the blood on my face she went bonkers, started yelling, and crying. I tried to tell her I was alright, just sore where the gun had kicked back or recoiled on me. Finally I got away from her. But not until she had wash me from head to toe! She wound a towel around my head and under my chin. I looked like the Mummy. She almost did more to me than the gun recoil!

I got to the back door of the house. There stood mom and Maw Maw G waiting for me. Granny C had phoned them. It took a bunch of explaining but I wiggled out of trouble for taking Dad's gun without his OK!

I made light of what happened and asked Maw Maw G if she would cook my birds and make some soft biscuits and thin gravy so I could chew without moving my sore jaws! She said "if you go hunting by yourself again, another part of you will be so sore you'll have to eat standing up."

As she went out the door, she picked up the two quail, called to Old Bob and said "come on with me I've got a biscuit for you, maybe a chewing bone too, for watching after that boy! He's going to give me gray hair." Old Bob walked beside her, wagging his tail and barking, as if to say to her "for a biscuit and a chewing bone, I'll do it anytime!"

THE OLD WHITE CHURCH

The meeting place for the schemes and pranks that we planned was the Old White Church.

Long abandoned, for whatever reasons, the building was used for mostly basketball games. Someone nailed a goal to the wall on each end of the church.

The location of the building was in the southeast corner of the crossroads where the Hunters lived. Stories of ghost or goblins and the people they carried off were many! Several times candles were seen burning inside the building or on the sill of a window frame. The shape or a shadow of what appeared to be a person could be seen when the light was giving off by the candles!

There were many stories about the old church. Particularly scary stories were told on the porch of the Old Store at Halloween. The wildest story was about a casket being under the floor and a body jumping out to grab anyone that disturbed the casket!

Willie D was always jumping out of places in the old church trying to scare Dink, Rabbit, Ollie Bay and me. He had found a hole in the floor, unknown to any of us goobers. He put some boards over the hole and waited. A pickup game was started. Willie played like he was sick and didn't play.

About ten minutes later Dink and Rabbit were scuffling over a loose ball near the boards over the hole in the floor! All of a sudden the boards flew through the air and a loud "GOTCHA" was shouted and out of the floor came Willie D. Rabbit and Dink tripped over one another, landing butt first on the old floor. The floor was just too rotten to hold up their weight. There they hung, arms and legs on the floor, with their rear end through the floor! Both were yelling for Help, Ollie Bay and me pulled Dink out of his demise first, because Rabbit was a bit heavier, about 35 pounds!! It would take some special planning to extract the Rabbit from his hole! I was trying to tell the gang how we could get Rabbit out of the floor. Since I was the only one willing to try this idea, all the gang said go for it hoping it wouldn't work!!

I slipped under the floor. Dink and Ollie Bay stood on each side of him and pulled him up. I crawled under his rear end and use my back to push him up!

Together, we got him out of the floor. Rabbit was laying on his stomach trying to catch his breath. I stood up through the hole in the floor and smacked Rabbit on the butt as I yelled "it worked". The thanks I got, Rabbit cut loose a roaring blast of gas that would make any skunk jealous! To a thunderous roar of laughter, from everyone above the floor, I slumped under the floor and crawled out into the churchyard, gasping for air! Such was the thanks for rescuing a goober!

Willie Dee and Bernie were the older, more experienced pranksters. They added spice to tricks that were sprung upon our victims. One of Willie Dee's advantages was an uncanny ability to improvise. Bernie just tagged along. To improvise was Willie D's claim to fame.

Like that night in the barn when Willie took the old telephone apart, the kind with the earpiece that hung in the u shaped arm. The arm extended out of the side of the stem, that had the part you spoke into on top of the stem. He was trying to make a speaker for a radio! But the earpiece of the phone was dry-rotted and produced only static! Same thing with the speaker of the radio, dry rot! The sounds needed a material that would vibrate. He tried cardboard but it was too rigid and thick. Then he used wood. Then silk, wool, cotton, even cheese clothe but still not enough vibration to hear sounds clearly. Finally he took Uncle C's tin snips and cut the top of a Quaker State motor oil can into the shape of the old earpiece. Bingo, the radio had a speaker that produced clear sound, the earpiece! Then he worked on the part of the phone that you spoke into to create a second speaker.

He had no equal in design of costumes, especially around Halloween and Harvest Festivals! He loved the horror movies made by Lon Chaney and Boris Karloff, such as the Mummy, Frankenstein, or the Werewolf. He could sound like those monsters, and his outfits, made of cheese clothe, candle wax and the hair from an animal were very scary! He made extended arms and fingers. To create screams from the ones on a hayride, a finger or arm would fall off and he'd squeeze a small bottle of red colored water, to make it appear to bleed from that body part! The best part was when the girls screamed and huddled closer to some guy on the ride.

Hayrides usually started with a spooky ghost story or a tale of strange things happening at a building, cemetery, or lonely stretch of a certain road. Then the driver of the wagon made sure the ride slowed to a crawl at certain locations! That's when the ghost and goblins always jumped out of the woods, old church, old barn or even a ditch, trying to scare the pants off someone!

Probably the wildest trick was the old casket and ghostly creature he and Bernie planned for one of the hayride groups to discover!

The hayride left Old Tom's store around dark thirty. That's half an hour after dark for those who can't tell time! The wagon driver was Rabbit's great uncle Shep. Shep played his part well. His voice was like Pontiac cars, it created excitement. We took turns punching him in he ribs. His response was a high-pitched squeal. Sometimes it would scare the horses. The sudden jerk of the wagon could cause some of the hay to fall off. The wagon would stop and the riders would put the hay back in the wagon. Also this was the signal for Willie Dee and Bernie to do their acting.

The ride carried us past Big Hub, little Bill, and Big Lu's house. Then up the hill by Uncle Pete and Granny C's house, everyone yelled to them as they sat on their porch. Ole Doc Tynch's medicine building was next about a half a mile down the road. He had passed away years ago but stories about him and his curing methods were many. Some were scary and others about lessons in life. Next we passed the spooky woods at Booger Hollow. When the wind blew through the trees a person could see anything he could imagine; Chief Crazy Horse chasing General Custer and his horse Dan, or ghosts dancing on every limb of a tree. Anything your mind desired.

The next scary spot was Ole Hoss' place. If he was drunk he would hide in his barn and stagger out, fire his shotgun and shout cuss words at the wagon.

Passing by Mr. Lawton B's pond was fun cause there were frogs and other varmints making noise that caused the girls to get closer to us guys! From here we would pass the Ole Bell at The Black Oak Cemetery!

Those on the ride included the Falstaff sisters, Go and Go-Go, the Brute sisters, Half a Ton and Won Ton, best two blockers in any football game! Next were the Applebum sisters, Kitt who was the oldest. She was the sweetest and most loyal friend I had in school at Tenbroeck. She was 2 or 3 years older than me and her sister, Boom-boom who was my classmate for 6 years. Little Purr got to go on this hayride, because big sister Peg convinced their Mom it was well chaperoned! Was Olli Bay fired up? If he had worn lipstick, the smile on his face would have gotten on both earlobes! Me, Dink, and Rabbit were just plain dumb when it came to girls! But we were in good hands as the Falstaff sisters tackled me and Dink. Go would have been penalized for holding, grabbing, and backfield in motion. I was the receiver and I declined the penalty! The other sister, GoGo, rushed Dink and sacked his for a 10 yard gain. "She can tackle me anytime!" yelled Dink. The Brute sisters took turns on Rabbit until he started farting and laughing! It got worse the more he laughed the more gas he passed.

Dudt and Peg were in the left corner and Ollie Bay and Little Purr were at the back of the wagon. The riders settled down as the bumps of the dirt road to Black Oak Cemetery became less frequent. Old Shep began to tell a story of the visitor to the Church bell in the spot where the old building was before it burnt. The bell would ring but no one was around it.

Old Shep would grasp for words to describe happenings in the story. His hesitations made the scary parts believable! The sounds of twigs snapping or leaves fluttering helped expectations rise! Then as the wagon full of riders went silent the BELL rang three times. A ghastly figure came from the graveyard and jumped on the step at the back of the wagon! Swinging an extra arm and slinging cold, wet fluid at everyone, the girls, all screaming, one or two crying, got even closer to the guys. Old Shep yelled, "time to go" and "get up" at the horses all in one breathe! The ghastly visitor jumped off the wagon, disappearing into the old graveyard, dragging an open casket and howling at the moon.

Old Shep made the right turns and each girl got off the hayride at their home. The guys were disappointed but we had fun. The trip back to Ole Tom's store had one more stop, the Old White Church. More than one guy wanted to stop to go to the bathroom. Since we had cleared around the building a couple of weeks ago, the wagon could pull off the dirt road near the front entrance. Then if a car should come by, it could get by the wagon!

We climbed off the hay and hurried to the back of the church. The moon, covered by clouds, began to inch out of the clouds, brighten the night. The full moon was about to help create some excitement! Each of us stood with our back to the crowd, finishing our appointment with nature, up walks Willie D and Bernie. Talk was about how scary the act on the wagon was, plus how chilling the sound of the bell ringing made some of the riders feel! As we made our way toward the wagon a LIGHT, Not the MOON brightened the inside of the Old White church! A crashing sound was made as a casket slid from a window frame and leaned against the building! The lid of the casket opened and an eerie figure covered in cheese clothe stumbled toward us! We all looked toward Willie D and Bernie, but it wasn't them after us! Who or What was it? I don't know what happened next. I found myself breathing hard and leaning against someone else gasping for air, too!

The four of us Dink, Rabbit, Tater, and Ollie Bay were sitting on the bench at Ole Tom's store. We took a look around the area trying to get an idea of what had scared the snot out of us!! It wasn't Willie Dee or Bernie, they were with us. Then who could it have been? Call us chicken or afraid of everything that night but the 4 of us walked to my house very close together and quickly also! We also locked the door and left a light on in my room. It wasn't easy but the 3 Goobers and a Nut slept in my regular size bed proving to all that we were close friends!

Mom woke me about daylight. Not trying to arouse the others, I bumped Ollie Bay and made a sign to be quiet but follow me. We followed Mom to the front porch. As she pointed across the woods towards the Hunters house we could see lots of blacken smoke curl up. The smoke was coming from a building on fire at the Hunters crossroads. "I hope its not Big Hub's house" said Rabbit and Dink at the same time. They began some kind of weird superstitious act to avoid bad luck from saying the something at the same time!

The phone rang and we all jumped like something had a hold on each of us! It was Aunt B wanting to know if Dink was there. She said there was a man from the fire marshals bureau wanting to talk to all of us guys! She told mom that the Old White Church was almost gone. It had caught fire in the night and the fire marshal was letting it burn out before his investigation began.

Nothing much was ever said after the fire marshal ask if we knew who the people were that night inside the church? How could we know, we were running too fast to ask for names!

GET THEM DARN GOATS OUTTA MY GARDEN

I would be in a tight situation if I needed to give a reason for writing this story! Let's just say the truth had to be stretched to Git 'er done!

Somewhere about 1948 along comes a baby boy that never had a chance to grow up correctly! The reasons, my brother, 9 years older, my sister, 13 years older, an aunt, 14 years older, and then there was Hawk, my firstest and worstest cousin! He never passed up an opportunity to play a prank on someone.

I guess he found the younger brother he never had, in me!

I was the only baby in our family for 5 years. I always got my way or it seemed so! Until Dink and Rabbit got here and aged enough for me to teach them what I endured from Hawk and Butch, my brother, plus Cooter, my sister, and the rest of the community jokesters!

Now to the Hawk, the Pride of Uncle J. Hill's nephews! Uncle Jay was a traveling showman and all around character. So naturally, Hawk took to him and anything he did with zest!

Uncle J owned a monkey! Maybe that's where Hawk got all those pranks!

Hawk joined the Air Force and he wasn't beyond using that to spring into action on some unknowing soul!

I had just graduated in 1966 and there was a phone call from a military person to me. Here I am 17, stupid and know it all, talking to a recruiter. He's giving me the hard sell about being drafted. I'm getting all ripped and mad, trying to tell him I want to go to college. He's puttin' all these figures and reasons I'd be better off in the service! That darn Rabbit was laughing at me and how mad I was about the questions the recruiter was asking me. Trying to get him to shut up, swing my arms and putting a finger across my lips for him to be quiet didn't work. When the recruiter ask me "if I had ever busted my ass on the bank of the Town Creek at the Nick Hale swimming hole!" I knew I'd been had! It was Hawk, laughing so hard he couldn't talk to me. I'm mad as an old wet hen, and can't think of what to say next, when I recognize his voice. He just called to say he would have come to my graduation, but Salt Lake City, Utah was too far away to come for an hour or so of diplomas being given out and 3 or 4 speeches by people he didn't know!

I think the time he called my sister in Beeville, Texas, demanding that she get her "darn goats outta his garden," was his finest hour. He talked about 2 minutes, hung up, called again, and told her to come and get her goats! Sis was yelling "I ain't got any goats." He hung up and called again. She invited him over and hung up on Hawk. What she did next scared her daughters so much they called their Dad (Soupy) at work! Little Bell yelled "Momma's got a ball bat and is sitting on the porch waiting for some man to come over and give her our goats that have eat his flower garden!" Then Lil' Bell asked, "Do we have goats? I want to feed them!"

With a huge laugh he told her to put my sister on the phone. He explained to her that this was planned by him and Hawk! She wasn't amused! She hung up, went back to the porch and wait for...not Hawk, but for Soupy! I'll get one of them she mumbled as she sat down to wait with bat in hand!

The Goobers Put Their Training into Action

It was the last week of May, school was out, and the Goobers caught me with my back turned! That's a cheap excuse for a fib. I was asleep! I had just finished my sophomore year in college! Knowing that I wouldn't be going to class for a while, I crashed at Maw Maw G's. I had parked the piece of scrap iron, it was impersonating a car, just outside the back bedroom I used when I was home from school!

Dink and Rabbit were on their way to the Junior high school to try to get a summer job.

Dink always said "I ain't gonna be no farmer!"

Rabbit would laugh and ask, "whatcha gonna do, fish for a living?"

Dinks reply was a Three Stooges move, a tap to

back of Rabbit's neck and head, then dodge as Rabbit tried to return fire! Both stopped in their tracks when they saw my scrap iron impersonator, the Tater Bug, as those two called the 65 hatchback VW I drove! It was a gas saver but the strange little things that went wrong with the car caused a lifetime of disgust over the cost for repairing the car. Those two removed the bucket seats, the carpet, the back seat, the spare tire and jack, plus, all my traveling necessities (ball glove, cleats, extra underwear—clean and used, etc!) Then they deposited these things in a couple of Maw Maw's apple trees!

I wake up to this crazy sound of roosters crowing and the theme of the Pink Panther blaring from the speakers of my car! Gosh, what a site to see! Me half asleep, hair askew, (good thing I sleep in coaching shorts), but no shirt, bare footed and trying to rub the sleep out of my eyes! As I looked around for the sounds that had stirred me from my dreams, I heard two cackling sounds made by two soon to be roasted goobers, if I can catch them! They were sitting against the wall of Pony J's grain shelling building, pointing and giggling at me! All I could think of was to throw something at those two. I gathered as many green apples as I could reach on the tree and chunked them at Rabbit and Dink. After I threw all those, I used the ones lying on the ground. I must have bumped the apple tree, because as I stumbled toward the house, parts of the inside of my car fell from the limbs. A head rest dropped in front of me and the console fell behind me! As I dodged those parts, the carpet came out of the tree, covering me like a blanket, knocking me to the ground! I scrambled to my feet, looking for those two "goobers". They were gone! Drat! Give me time, I'll get them, I was thinking, as I walked carrying my car floor mats and the other car parts back to be reassembled.

I took about two hours to replace all the parts of my scrap iron pile on wheels! As you can tell by now I really like that...uh car! I drove it but never again would that brand of products name cross my lips in a positive way. I hate the name, to this day, of that car!!

Let's get back to the threat of revenge that I was about to try on the Dinkster and the Rabbit! My loyal side kick, Ollie Bay, was driving a truck and trailer that hauled cars from up north that his dad and uncle fixed and re-sold. That meant finding rookies to replace a veteran prankster.

First, I had to involve the Falstaff sister's, Go and Go-Go, in the prank I had planned. I bribed them by taking them swimming at Nick Hale's on Town Creek! Plus, they knew I wouldn't tell anyone they went skinny dippin' while we were there. That's how they could have a tan so that no tan lines could be seen on them. None of the guys knew it but each girl had a birth mark shaped like an "i" on her body part only known to me! Besides this pair of friends was as close to me as my sister, plus, they loved to pull pranks on anyone!

Go-Go, the older sister, wasn't above doing anything to anyone at anytime and the more mischievous the better she liked it! So she was the one to do the strong arm part and little Go would do the part requiring precise execution! Timing was the key to the gooberization of those two goobers! I was determined to nail them.

We pulled the scrap pile (car) under the back corner of Ole Toms store. The buildings floor joists were over 7 feet off the ground at the southeast corner. The support piers, the floor joist were on, had about 10 feet between them, making a perfect hiding place for the pile of bolts(car)! If the "goobers," Dink and Rabbit, saw it they might suspect something was about to happen. The girls went inside and chatted with Hay-zella while I waited near the drink box watching for our prey!

I signaled the girls to get set! I was getting in place to take pictures of what was about to occur. Go-Go hid by the counter where cheese, and meats were cut. It was near the drink box, which was perfect, because the first place Dink and Rabbit went was the drink box for an RC or a Double Cola. Then reach across the drink box to get a pack of peanuts or moon pie.

Little Go was behind the counter where cloth was measured and cut. It was just a few feet from where Rabbit would turn and face her.

Dink opened the screen and entered as if he owned the world, announcing that the professor of education, at Tenbroeck School, had hired two goobers for the summer.

Rabbit entered and said, "I need something to drink, it's hot!"

They faced the drink box and lifted the lid. Each removed a drink, before reaching across the lid for the snacks on the shelf behind the drink box.

The girls sprang into action! Go-Go grabbed Dinks pants and yanked them down to his knees. She then smacked his bare butt with her hand, and dashed out the front screen door, laughing and clapping her hands! While Dink was pulling his pants up and trying to hold on to his drink, I took a picture. Hay-zella was stuttering and trying to yell but nothing came out of her mouth. Must have been the foam that stopped the words, because she was spewing like a volcano! Several of the older folks inside the store were howling with laughter! As I wound the film to get another shot, the younger sister, Go, sprang from her spot and as Rabbit turned, laughing at Dink, she wrapped her arms around his neck and planted the biggest slobber knocker of a kiss on Rabbit, I had ever seen!

As I snapped the last picture, Dink got his pants up and Rabbit, leaning on the drink box, his face fire engine red, looked at Dink and said, "he finally got us!"

Dink replied, "yeah, but it took three of them to do it."

Rabbit came back with "well, we've been double teaming Tater, so I guess we deserve it!"

At the back of the store we jumped into my car, did I say car? Anyway, we drove around to the front of Ole Tom's Store expecting to see a couple of mad "goobers"; those two were laughing, drinking and eating, and pointing at us.

The girls yelled, "come on let's go to the creek!"

Those "goobers" ran to the junk pile...uh car, Dink crawled in the backseat and both the girls went after him. They went over the seat and the laughter and giggling set in.

Rabbit took the front seat, sipped his drink, turned to me, smiled and said, "you got us."

Pulling on to the road toward the swimming hole, I laughed and said, "yeah we did, but it was because I had good help" as I looked in the rear view mirror.

Go and Go-Go were all excited yelling, "yes, yes, yes" over Dinks "no, no, no!"

They wanted to see if the hand print was still on Dink's butt!

As we made our way to the creek, little Go grabbed Rabbit and laid another slobber knocker of a kiss on him and watch him turn red again. I just smiled and enjoyed my revenge! The two goobers were enjoying it, too!

Maybe I'll make the girls full time members of the "goobers". I think they would like that!

I know I would!!

THE POLE FOLLOWS US HOME!

One can never have enough friends. So, when Rabbit and Dink tried out for the GSCC baseball team they met a redheaded Polish peacock that we nicknamed Polagora. It was an instant blend, his ability to be lead, our insane schemes, his distinct laugh after the prank, and the fun we enjoyed pulling each prank.

Being from Birmingham, Polagora didn't get to enjoy the finer things that growing up in the country provides. Things like homegrown green onions, Pinto beans cooked with a piece of streak of lean meat, and fresh baked pones of cornbread. Aunt B's corn meal had been fresh ground at the Gristmill on the creek. The meat seasons the beans with a smoke house cured flavor. This will cause ones tongue to rub a blister on the roof of your mouth trying to get another taste of the previous mouth full. The taste buds seem to get impatient once you swallow! Howling for the next bite of that cool, crisp, flavorful onion laced with more beans and cornbread, just waiting for a huge gulp of ice-cold sweet tea!

Those vittles, a southern term for food, and a fishing trip, were rewards Polagora earned for all the pranks we played on him!!

The first stop was at the ponds at Tenbroeck, where Dink and my grandmother's home were located. We caught several bluegill and a few small bass. The bluegill we would keep but the bass we released to allow them to grow.

Next, we tried Big Luke's pond. The fish, mostly bass, were bigger than the ones caught at Tenbroeck, but nobody wanted to clean them so we released them back into the pond.

The last stop was "Tipsy Ole Boots" pond. Getting to his pond required stealth and cunning. He wouldn't allow anyone to fish his pond because we had to climb his fence to get to his pond. He claimed we bent his fence and his pigs got out! We just waited until he went to the Old Store, at the cross roads, about a mile away and then use the gate next to the barn. He always went at the same time each day, 11:00 a.m.

He would drink a small Coca Cola and smoke a half a pack of Camel cigarettes, while chatting with whomever was around the store. If there were several men at the store he swapped stories and got caught up on the local gossip, uh news! And, have a second Coke, and smoke another ten or twelve Camel's!

When he left his house, he would leave his yard without regard to where his driveway was! His new Chevy truck was bouncing, as he crossed the ditch or if he ran off the driveway, he would gun the motor and release the clutch. The tires would dig into dirt, spin, and sling anything they touched flying! Leaving a trail of dust so thick a blind man could follow it by touching the particles in the air! He could be seen for half a mile going or come. His return trail of dust gave us time to get out of his pasture.

Polagora hooked the biggest fish at Tipsy Ole Boot's pond that day. He didn't know that Ole Boots had tried to eliminate the larger bass, in his pond, by shooting them with a shotgun. Ole Boots was just trying to give the smaller fish a chance to grow up!

Polagora was fishing the side of the pond next to John and Fred T's creek. The pond spillway had lots of cattails growing around its edge where the runoff water emptied into the creek. The cattails provided a very good place to hide for the fish we had nicknamed "Buck Shot." Dink and Rabbit had hooked the old bass a number of times, but always released it. None of us Goobers were going to take away the glow on Polagora face by getting him to return his catch.

When he hooked the fish, he lost his balance and slipped into the edge of the pond. Somehow he regained his balance and got back on the bank. Wet up to his waist, Polagora kept the hook anchored in the big bass's mouth. In between his whooping and yelling, our laughing at the moves Polagora made, he landed the huge bass.

Always leery of getting caught by Tipsy Ole Boots, I had one eye on the dirt road and the other on the fun Polagora was having.

I caught sight of a dust cloud being made by a farm truck! It was probably Ole Boots, headed home to watch his soap opera's, plus catch us at his pond! The three of us began to yell to Polagora, that trouble was headed our way!

Rabbit shouted, "land that bass and get in the creek. Follow it to the bridge and we'll pick you up!"

The three of us, Tater, Rabbit, and Dink grabbed

all the fishing gear and tossed it in Tater's 1973 HATCHBACK NOVA SS and headed down the field road to meet Polagora on the backside of Ole Boots woods.

We barely got into the cover of the kudzu and boxwood, when Tipsy Ole Boots drove into his yard. His dog must have smelled us! It was jumping all over Ole Boots and the truck!

Ole Boots was hollering and cussing a blue streak at the dog! Slapping at the dog, trying to park his truck, he missed his brakes, and his mobile home by inches, before coming to a stop in the ditch that divided his yard and the field road we were hiding on! Still mad at his dog, Ole Boots didn't hear the roar of my dual exhausts as we puttered through the woods and out the backside of his land!

We met Polagora at the bridge, loaded his gear and his trophy, "Ole Buck Shot" in the car and headed to Aunt B's for something to eat. Jerry Clower would have compared the meal to the way a Blue Tick hound would strut after he had won the Blue Ribbon at a dog show! Ain't nothin' better than Aunt B's home cooking!

She was prepared for me, Dink and Rabbit! But she couldn't believe the Polagora's appetite! We ate a four-quart pressure cooker full of pinto beans, two garden onions, each about the size of a softball and cut into quarters, three pones of cornbread, cooked in a number 10 sized skillet. All of this was washed down with two gallons of ice-cold sweet tea.

Naturally, three 18 year old boys and one, suppose to be, adult male of 23, all single and goofy in actions, are about to show their immaturity.

On Monday night several guys had gathered at Dink and Rabbit's apartment to watch a baseball game. Jokes and tall tales were told. Each guy trying to top the previous story!

With perfect timing Rabbit yelled, "Quiet!"

As the National Anthem was being played, he raised his leg and kept time, with bubbles of gas for the first ten notes! After the laughter and roaring approval of his actions, had subsided, these weird sounds of gagging, gasping and coughing could be heard! Noses dripped, eyes developed tear drops, and guys were crawling out of the room! The Rabbit won that bull shooting session by a NOSE! There wasn't anyone around to nose him out!!

This was about a good friend, ball player and a good man whose life was cut short by a car wreck! We miss you Polagora and would love to take you on a snipe hunt, sit by a campfire, and swap lies and stories!

Maybe we can all go fishing together, the four of us, and the greatest fisherman of all, in the rivers of Glory one Fine Day!